Who snatched Betty Sprot?

Betty was loud, lively, not quite three years old and definitely more little girl than most ordinary mothers could cope with. But Mrs. Sprot was no ordinary mother, and she coped quite nicely— that is until little Betty got herself kidnapped. Then Mrs. Sprot got herself a gun, and two faceless initials like N and M turned out to be very important matters of life and death.

N or M?

AGATHA CHRISTIE

A DELL BOOK

Published by
DELL PUBLISHING CO., INC.
750 Third Avenue
New York, New York 10017

Reprinted by arrangement with
Dodd, Mead & Company
New York, New York
Printed in the U.S.A.
Previous Dell Edition #6254
New Dell Edition
First printing—January 1971

1

Tommy Beresford removed his overcoat in the hall of the flat. He hung it up with some care, taking time over it. His hat went carefully on the next peg.

He squared his shoulders, affixed a resolute smile to his face and walked into the sitting room where his wife sat knitting a Balaclava helmet in khaki wool.

Mrs. Beresford gave him a quick glance and then busied herself by knitting at a furious rate. She said after a minute or two:

"Any news in the evening paper?"

Tommy said:

"The Blitzkrieg is coming, hurray, hurray! Things look bad in France."

Tuppence said:

"It's a depressing world at the moment."

There was a pause and then Tommy said:

"Well, why don't you ask? No need to be so damned tactful."

"I know," admitted Tuppence. "There is something about conscious tact that is very irritating. But then it irritates you if I do ask. And anyway I don't *need* to ask. It's written all over you."

"I wasn't conscious of looking a Dismal Desmond."

"No, darling," said Tuppence. "You had a kind of nailed to the mast smile which was one of the most heart-rending things I have ever seen."

Tommy said with a grin:

"No, was it really as bad as all that?"

"And more! Well, come on, out with it. Nothing doing?"

"Nothing doing. They don't want me in any capacity. I tell you, Tuppence, it's pretty thick when a man of forty-six is made to feel like a doddering grandfather. Army, Navy, Air Force, Foreign Office, one and all say the same thing—I'm too old. I *may* be required later."

Tuppence said:

"Well, it's the same for me. They don't want people of my age for nursing—no, thank you. Nor for anything else. They'd rather have a fluffy chit who's never seen a wound, or sterilized a dressing, than they would have me who worked for three years, 1915 to 1918, in various capacities, nurse in the surgical ward and operating theatre, driver of a trade delivery van and later of a General. This, that and the other—all, I assert firmly, with conspicuous success. And now I'm a poor, pushing, tiresome, middle-aged woman who won't sit at home quietly and knit as she ought to do."

Tommy said gloomily:

"This War is Hell."

"It's bad enough having a war," said Tuppence, "but not being allowed to do anything in it just puts the lid on."

Tommy said consolingly:

"Well, at any rate Deborah has got a job."

Deborah's mother said:

"Oh, she's all right. I expect she's good at it, too. But I still think, Tommy, that I could hold my own with Deborah."

Tommy grinned.

"She wouldn't think so."

Tuppence said:

"Daughters can be very trying. Especially when they *will* be so kind to you."

Tommy murmured:

"The way young Derek makes allowances for me is sometimes rather hard to bear. That 'poor old Dad' look in his eye."

"In fact," said Tuppence, "our children, although quite adorable, are also quite maddening."

But at the mention of the twins, Derek and Deborah, her eyes were very tender.

"I suppose," said Tommy thoughtfully, "that it's always

hard for people themselves to realize that they're getting middle-aged and past doing things."

Tuppence gave a snort of rage, tossed her glossy dark head and sent her ball of khaki wool spinning from her lap.

"Are we past doing things? *Are* we? Or is it only that everyone keeps insinuating that we are. Sometimes I feel that we never were any use."

"Quite likely," said Tommy.

"Perhaps so. But at any rate we did once feel important. And now I'm beginning to feel that all that never really happened. Did it happen, Tommy? Is it true that you were once crashed on the head and kidnapped by German agents? Is it true that we once tracked down a dangerous criminal—and got him? Is it true that we rescued a girl and got hold of important secret papers, and were practically thanked by a grateful country? Us! You and me! Despised, unwanted Mr. and Mrs. Beresford."

"Now, dry up, darling. All this does no good."

"All the same," said Tuppence, blinking back a tear. "I'm disappointed in our Mr. Carter."

"He wrote us a very nice letter."

"He didn't *do* anything—he didn't even hold out any hope."

"Well, he's out of it all nowadays. Like us. He's quite old. Lives in Scotland and fishes."

Tuppence said wistfully:

"They might have let us do *something* in the Intelligence."

"Perhaps we couldn't," said Tommy. "Perhaps, nowadays, we wouldn't have the nerve."

"I wonder," said Tuppence. "One feels just the same. But perhaps, as you say, when it came to the point—"

She sighed. She said:

"I wish we could find a job of some kind. It's so rotten when one has so much time to think."

Her eyes rested just for a minute on the photograph of the very young man in Air Force uniform, with the wide grinning smile so like Tommy's.

Tommy said:

"It's worse for a man. Women can knit, after all—and do up parcels and help at canteens."

Tuppence said:

"I can do all that twenty years from now. I'm not old enough to be content with that. I'm neither one thing nor the other."

The front door bell rang. Tuppence got up. The flat was a small service one.

She opened the door to find a broad-shouldered man with a big fair moustache and a cheerful red face, standing on the mat.

His glance, a quick one, took her in as he asked in a pleasant voice:

"Are you Mrs. Beresford?"

"Yes."

"My name's Grant. I'm a friend of Lord Easthampton's. He suggested I should look you and your husband up."

"Oh, how nice, do come in."

She preceded him into the sitting room.

"My husband, er—Captain—"

"Mr."

"Mr. Grant. He's a friend of Mr. Car— of Lord Easthampton's."

The old *nom de guerre* of the former Chief of the Intelligence, "Mr. Carter," always came more easily to her lips than their old friend's proper title.

For few minutes the three talked happily together. Grant was an attractive person with an easy manner.

Presently Tuppence left the room. She returned a few minutes later with the sherry and some glasses.

After a few minutes, when a pause came, Mr. Grant said to Tommy:

"I hear you're looking for a job, Beresford?"

An eager light came into Tommy's eye.

"Yes, indeed. You don't mean—"

Grant laughed, and shook his head.

"Oh, nothing of that kind. No, I'm afraid that has to be left to the young active men—or to those who've been at it for years. The only things I can suggest are rather stodgy, I'm afraid. Office work. Filing papers. Tying them up in red tape and pigeon-holing them. That sort of thing."

Tommy's face fell.

"Oh, I see!"

Grant said encouragingly:

"Oh, well, it's better than nothing. Anyway, come and see me at my office one day. Ministry of Requirements. Room 22. We'll fix you up with something."

The telephone rang. Tuppence picked up the receiver.

"Hullo—yes—*what?*" A squeaky voice spoke agitatedly from the other end. Tuppence's face changed. "When? Oh, my dear—of course—I'll come over right away. . . ."

She put back the receiver.

She said to Tommy:

"That was Maureen."

"I thought so—I recognized her voice from here."

Tuppence explained breathlessly:

"I'm so sorry, Mr. Grant. But I must go round to this friend of mine. She's fallen and twisted her ankle and there's no one with her but her little girl, so I must go round and fix up things for her and get hold of someone to come in and look after her. Do forgive me."

"Of course, Mrs. Beresford, I quite understand."

Tuppence smiled at him, picked up a coat which had been lying over the sofa, slipped her arms into it and hurried out. The flat door banged.

Tommy poured out another glass of sherry for his guest.

"Don't go yet," he said.

"Thank you." The other accepted the glass. He sipped it for a moment in silence. Then he said: "In a way, you know, your wife's being called away is a fortunate occurrence. It will save time."

Tommy stared.

"I don't understand."

Grant said deliberately:

"You see, Beresford, if you had come to see me at the Ministry, I was empowered to put a certain proposition before you."

The colour came slowly up in Tommy's freckled face. He said:

"You don't mean—"

Grant nodded.

"Easthampton suggested you," he said. "He told us you were the man for the job."

Tommy gave a deep sigh.

"Tell me," he said.

"This is strictly confidential, of course."

Tommy nodded.

"Not even your wife must know. You understand?"

"Very well—if you say so. But we worked together before."

"Yes, I know. But this proposition is solely for you."

"I see. All right."

"Ostensibly you will be offered work—as I said just now —office work—in a branch of the Ministry functioning in Scotland—in a prohibited area where your wife cannot accompany you. Actually you will be somewhere very different."

Tommy merely waited.

Grant said:

"You've read in the newspapers of the Fifth Column? You know, roughly at any rate, just what that term implies."

Tommy murmured:

"The enemy within."

"Exactly. This war, Beresford, started in an optimistic spirit. Oh, I don't mean the people who really knew—we've known all along what we were up against—the efficiency of the enemy, his aerial strength, his deadly determination, and the co-ordination of his well-planned war machine. I mean the people as a whole. The good-hearted, muddle-headed democratic fellow who believes what he wants to believe— that Germany will crack up, that she's on the verge of revolution, that her weapons of war are made of tin and that her men are so underfed that they'll fall down if they try to march—all that sort of stuff. Wishful thinking, as the saying goes.

"Well, the war didn't go that way. It started badly and it went on worse. The men were all right—the men on the battleships and in the planes and in the dugouts. But there was mismanagement and unpreparedness—the defects, perhaps, of our qualities. We don't want war, haven't considered it seriously, weren't good at preparing for it.

"The worst of that is over. We've corrected our mistakes, we're slowly getting the right men in the right places. We're beginning to run the war as it should be run—and we can win the war—make no mistake about that—but only if we don't lose it first. And the danger of losing it comes, not from outside—not from the might of Germany's bombers, not from her seizure of neutral countries and fresh vantage points from which to attack—but from within. Our danger is the danger of Troy—the wooden horse within our walls. Call it the Fifth Column if you like. It is here, among us. Men and women, some of them highly placed, some of them obscure, but all believing genuinely in the Nazi aim and the Nazi creed and desiring to substitute that sternly efficient creed for the muddled easy-going liberty of our democratic institutions."

Grant leaned forward. He said, still in that same pleasant unemotional voice:

"And we don't know who they are. . . ."

Tommy said: "But surely—"

Grant said, with a touch of impatience:

"Oh, we can round up the small fry. That's easy enough. But it's the others. We know about them. We know that there are at least two highly placed in the Admiralty—that one must be a member of General G——'s staff—that there are three or more in the Air Force, and that two, at least, are members of the Intelligence, know Cabinet secrets. We know that because it must be so from the way things have happened. The leakage—a leakage from the top—of information to the enemy, shows us that."

Tommy said helplessly, his pleasant face perplexed:

"But what good should I be to you? I don't know any of these people."

Grant nodded.

"Exactly. You don't know any of them—*and they don't know you.*"

He paused to let it sink in and then went on.

"These people, these high up people, know most of our lot. Information can't be very well refused to them. I was at my wits' end. I went to Easthampton. He's out of it all now

—a sick man—but his brain's the best I've ever known. He thought of you. Nearly twenty years since you worked for the Department. Name quite unconnected with it. Your face not known. What do you say—will you take it on?"

Tommy's face was almost split in two by the magnitude of his ecstatic grin.

"Take it on? You bet I'll take it on. Though I can't see how I can be of any use. I'm just a blasted amateur."

"My dear Beresford, amateur status is just what is needed. The professional is handicapped here. You'll take on in place of the best man we had or are likely to have."

Tommy looked a question. Grant nodded.

"Yes. Died in St. Bridget's Hospital last Tuesday. Run down by a lorry—only lived a few hours. Accident case—but it wasn't an accident."

Tommy said slowly: "I see."

Grant said quietly:

"And that's why we have reason to believe that Farquhar was on to something—that he was getting somewhere at last. By his death that wasn't an accident."

Tommy looked a question.

Grant went on:

"Unfortunately we know next to nothing of what he had discovered. Farquhar had been methodically following up one line after another. Most of them led nowhere."

Grant paused and then went on:

"Farquhar was unconscious until a few minutes before he died. Then he tried to say something. What he said was this: *N or M Song Susie.*"

"That," said Tommy, "doesn't seem very illuminating."

Grant smiled.

"A little more so than you might think. N or M, you see, is a term we have heard before. It refers to two of the most important and trusted German agents. We have come across their activities in other countries and we know just a little about them. It is their mission to organize a Fifth Column in foreign countries and to act as liaison officer between the country in question and Germany. N, we know, is a man. M is a woman. All we know about them is that these two are Hitler's most highly trusted agents and that in a code message we managed to decipher towards the beginning of the war there occurred this phrase—*Suggest N or M for England. Full powers*—"

"I see. And Farquhar—"

"As I see it, Farquhar must have got on the track of one or other of them. Unfortunately we don't know *which*. Song Susie sounds very cryptic—but Farquhar hadn't a high class French accent! There was a return ticket to Leahampton in his pocket which is suggestive. Leahampton is on the South coast—a budding Bournemouth or Torquay. Lots of private hotels and guest houses. Amongst them is one called *Sans Souci*—"

Tommy said again:

"Song Susie—Sans Souci—I see."

Grant said:

"Do you?"

"The idea is," Tommy said, "that I should go there and—well—ferret round."

"That *is* the idea."

Tommy's smile broke out again.

"A bit vague, isn't it?" he asked. "I don't even know what I'm looking for."

"And I can't tell you. I don't know. It's up to you."

Tommy sighed. He squared his shoulders.

"I can have a shot at it. But I'm not a very brainy sort of chap."

"You did pretty well in the old days, so I've heard."

"Oh, that was pure luck," said Tommy hastily.

"Well, luck is rather what we need."

Tommy considered a minute or two. Then he said:

"About this place, Sans Souci—"

Grant shrugged his shoulders.

"May be all a mare's nest. I can't tell. Farquhar may have been thinking of 'Sister Susie's sewing shirts for soldiers.' It's all guesswork."

"And Leahampton itself?"

"Just like any other of these places. There are rows of them. Old ladies, old Colonels, unimpeachable spinsters, dubious customers, fishy customers, a foreigner or two. In fact, a mixed bag."

Tommy said doubtfully:

"And N or M amongst them?"

"Not necessarily. Somebody, perhaps, who's in touch with N or M. But it's quite likely to be N or M themselves. It's an inconspicuous sort of place, a boarding-house at a seaside resort."

"You've no idea whether it's a man or a woman I've to look for?"

Grant shook his head.

Tommy said: "Well, I can but try."

"Good luck to your trying, Beresford. Now—to details—"

TWO

Half an hour later, when Tuppence broke in, panting and eager with curiosity, Tommy was alone, whistling in an armchair with a doubtful expression on his face.

"Well?" demanded Tuppence, throwing an infinity of feeling into the word.

"A job—of kinds."

"What kind?"

Tommy made a suitable grimace.

"Office work in the wilds of Scotland. Hush-hush and all that, but doesn't sound very thrilling."

"Both of us, or only you?"

"Only me, I'm afraid."

"Blast and curse you. How *could* our Mr. Carter be so mean?"

"I imagine they segregate the sexes in these jobs. Otherwise, too distracting for the mind."

"Is it coding—or code breaking? Is it like Deborah's job? Do be careful, Tommy; people go queer doing that and can't sleep; walk about all night groaning and repeating 978345286 or something like that and finally have nervous breakdowns and go into homes."

"Not me."

Tuppence said gloomily:

"I expect you will sooner or later. Can I come, too—not to work but just as a wife? Slippers in front of the fire and a hot meal at the end of the day?"

Tommy looked uncomfortable.

"Sorry, old thing. I *am* sorry. I hate leaving you——"

"But you feel you ought to go," murmured Tuppence reminiscently.

"After all," said Tommy feebly, "you can knit, you know."

"Knit?" said Tuppence. *"Knit?"*

Seizing her Balaclava helmet, she flung it on the ground.

"I hate khaki wool," said Tuppence, *"and* Navy wool *and* Air Force blue. I should like to knit something *magenta!"*

"It has a fine military sound," said Tommy. "Almost a suggestion of Blitzkrieg."

He felt definitely very unhappy. Tuppence, however, was a Spartan and played up well, admitting freely that of course he had to take the job and that it didn't *really* matter about her. She added that she had heard they wanted someone to scrub down the First Aid Post floors. She might possibly be found fit to do that.

Tommy departed for Aberdeen three days later. Tuppence saw him off at the station. Her eyes were bright and she blinked once or twice, but she kept resolutely cheerful.

Only as the train drew out of the station and Tommy saw the forlorn little figure walking away down the platform did he feel a lump in his own throat. War or no War he felt he was deserting Tuppence. . . .

He pulled himself together with an effort. Orders were orders.

Having duly arrived in Scotland, he took a train the next day to Manchester. On the third day a train deposited him at Leahampton. Here he went to the principal Hotel and on the following day made a tour of various private hotels and guest houses, seeing rooms and inquiring terms for a long stay.

Sans Souci was a dark red Victorian villa, set on the side of a hill with a good view over the sea from its upper windows. There was a slight smell of dust and cooking in the hall and the carpet was worn, but it compared quite favourably with some of the other establishments Tommy had seen. He interviewed the proprietress, Mrs. Perenna, in her office, a small untidy room with a large desk covered with loose papers.

Mrs. Perenna herself was rather untidy looking, a woman of middle-age with a large mop of fiercely curling black hair, some vaguely applied makeup and a determined smile showing a lot of very white teeth.

Tommy murmured a mention of his elderly cousin, Miss Meadowes, who had stayed at Sans Souci two years ago. Mrs. Perenna remembered Miss Meadowes quite well—such a dear old lady—at least perhaps not really old—very active and such a sense of humour.

Tommy agreed cautiously. There was, he knew, a real Miss Meadowes—the Department was careful about these points.

And how was dear Miss Meadowes?

Tommy explained sadly that Miss Meadowes was no more and Mrs. Perenna clicked her teeth sympathetically and made the proper noises and put on a correct mourning face.

She was soon talking volubly again. She had, she was sure, just the room that would suit Mr. Meadowes. A lovely sea view. She thought Mr. Meadowes was so right to want to get out of London. Very depressing nowadays, so she understood, and of course, after such a bad go of influenza—

Still talking, Mrs. Perenna led Tommy upstairs and showed him various bedrooms. She mentioned a weekly sum. Tommy displayed dismay. Mrs. Perenna explained that prices had risen so appallingly. Tommy explained that his income had unfortunately decreased and what with taxation and one thing and another—

Mrs. Perenna groaned and said:

"This terrible War—"

Tommy agreed and said that in his opinion that fellow Hitler ought to be hanged. A madman, that's what he was, a madman.

Mrs. Perenna agreed and said that what with rations and the difficulty the butchers had in getting the meat they wanted—and sometimes too much—and sweetbreads and liver practically disappeared, it all made housekeeping very difficult, but as Mr. Meadowes was a relation of Miss Meadowes, she would make it half a guinea less.

Tommy then beat a retreat with the promise to think it over and Mrs. Perenna pursued him to the gate, talking more volubly than ever and displaying an archness that Tommy found most alarming. She was, he admitted, quite a handsome woman in her way. He found himself wondering what her nationality was. Surely not quite English? The name was Spanish or Portuguese, but that would be her husband's nationality, not hers. She might, he thought, be Irish, though she had no brogue. But it would account for the vitality and the exuberance.

It was finally settled that Mr. Meadowes should move in the following day.

Tommy timed his arrival for six o'clock. Mrs. Perenna came out into the hall to greet him, threw a series of instructions about his luggage to an almost imbecile-looking maid, who goggled at Tommy with her mouth open, and then led him into what she called the lounge.

"I always introduce my guests," said Mrs. Perenna, beaming determinedly at the suspicious glares of five people. "This is our new arrival, Mr. Meadowes—Mrs. O'Rourke." A terrifying mountain of a woman with beady eyes and a moustache gave him a beaming smile.

"Major Bletchley." Major Bletchley eyed Tommy appraisingly and made a stiff inclination of the head.

"Mr. von Deinim." A young man, very stiff, fair-haired and blue-eyed, got up and bowed.

"Miss Minton." An elderly woman with a lot of beads, knitting with khaki wool, smiled and tittered.

"And Mrs. Blenkensop." More knitting—an untidy dark head which lifted from an absorbed contemplation of a Balaclava helmet.

Tommy held his breath; the room spun round.

Mrs. Blenkensop! Tuppence! By all that was impossible and unbelievable—Tuppence, calmly knitting in the lounge of Sans Souci.

Her eyes met his—polite uninterested stranger's eyes.

His admiration rose.

Tuppence!

2

How Tommy got through that evening he never quite knew. He dared not let his eyes stray too often in the direction of Mrs. Blenkensop. At dinner three more habitués of Sans Souci appeared—a middle-aged couple—Mr. and Mrs. Cayley and a young mother, Mrs. Sprot, who had come down with her baby girl from London and was clearly much bored by her enforced stay at Leahampton. She was placed next to Tommy and at intervals fixed him with a pair of pale gooseberry eyes and in a slightly adenoidal voice asked: "Don't you think it's really quite safe now? Everybody's going back, aren't they?"

Before Tommy could reply to these artless queries, his neighbor on the other side, the beaded lady, struck in: "What I say is one mustn't risk anything with children. Your sweet little Betty. You'd never forgive yourself and you know that Hitler has said the Blitzkrieg on England is coming quite soon now—and quite a new kind of gas, I believe."

Major Bletchley cut in sharply:

"Lot of nonsense talked about gas. The fellows won't waste time fiddling round with gas. High explosive and incendiary bombs. That's what was done in Spain."

The whole table plunged into the argument with gusto. Tuppence's voice, high pitched and slightly fatuous, piped out:

"My son Douglas says—"

"Douglas, indeed," thought Tommy. "Why Douglas, I should like to know."

After dinner, a pretentious meal of several meagre courses, all of which were equally tasteless, everyone drifted into the lounge. Knitting was resumed and Tommy was compelled to hear a long and extremely boring account of Major Bletchley's experiences on the North West Frontier.

The fair young man with the bright blue eyes went out, executing a little bow on the threshold of the room.

Major Bletchley broke off his narrative and administered a kind of dig in the ribs to Tommy.

"That fellow who's just gone out. He's a refugee. Got out of Germany about a month before the war."

"He's a German?"

"Yes. Not a Jew, either. His father got into trouble for criticizing the Nazi régime. Two of his brothers are in a concentration camp over there. This fellow got out just in time."

At this moment Tommy was taken possession of by Mrs. Cayley, who told him at interminable length all about her health. So absorbing was the subject to the narrator that it was close upon bedtime before Tommy could escape.

On the following morning Tommy rose early and strolled down to the front. He walked briskly to the pier and was returning along the esplanade when he spied a familiar figure coming in the other direction. Tommy raised his hat.

"Good morning," he said pleasantly. "Er—Mrs. Blenkensop, isn't it?"

There was no one within earshot. Tuppence replied:

"Dr. Livingstone to you."

"How on earth did you get here, Tuppence?" murmured Tommy. "It's a miracle—an absolute miracle."

"It's not a miracle at all—just brains."

"Your brains, I suppose?"

"You suppose rightly. You and your uppish Mr. Grant. I hope this will teach him a lesson."

"It certainly ought to," said Tommy. "Come on, Tuppence, tell me how you managed it. I'm simply devoured with curiosity."

"It was quite simple. The moment Grant talked of our Mr. Carter I guessed what was up. I knew it wouldn't be just some miserable office job. But his saying so showed me

that I wasn't going to be allowed in on this. So I resolved to
go one better. I went to fetch some sherry and, when I did,
I nipped down to the Browns' flat and rang up Maureen.
Told her to ring me up and what to say. She played up
loyally—nice high squeaky voice—you could hear what
she was saying all over the room. I did my stuff, registered
annoyance, compulsion, distressed friend, and rushed off
with every sign of vexation. Banged the hall door, carefully
remaining inside it, and slipped into the bedroom and eased
open the communicating door that's hidden by the tallboy."

"And you heard everything?"

"Everything," said Tuppence complacently.

Tommy said reproachfully:

"And you never let on."

"Certainly not. I wished to teach you a lesson. You and
your Mr. Grant."

"He's not exactly my Mr. Grant and I should say you
have taught him a lesson."

"Mr. Carter wouldn't have treated me so shabbily," said
Tuppence. "I don't think the Intelligence is anything like
what it was in our day."

Tommy said gravely:

"It will attain its former brilliance now we're back in it.
But why Blenkensop?"

"Why not?"

"It seems such an odd name to choose."

"It was the first one I thought of and it's handy for under-
clothes."

"What do you mean, Tuppence?"

"B, you idiot. B for Beresford, B for Blenkensop. Embroidered on my cami-knickers. Patricia Blenkensop. Prud-
ence Beresford. Why did you choose Meadowes? It's a silly
name."

"To begin with," said Tommy, "I don't have large B's
embroidered on my pants. And to continue, I didn't choose
it. I was told to call myself Meadowes. Mr. Meadowes is a
gentleman with a respectable past—all of which I've learned
by heart."

"Very nice," said Tuppence. "Are you married or single?"

"I'm a widower," said Tommy with dignity. "My wife died ten years ago at Singapore."

"Why at Singapore?"

"We've all got to die somewhere. What's wrong with Singapore?"

"Oh, nothing. It's probably a most suitable place to die. I'm a widow."

"Where did your husband die?"

"Does it matter? Probably in a nursing home. I rather fancy he died of cirrhosis of the liver."

"I see. A painful subject. And what about your son Douglas?"

"Douglas is in the Navy."

"So I heard last night."

"And I've got two other sons. Raymond is in the Air Force and Cyril, my baby, is in the Territorials."

"And suppose someone takes the trouble to check up on these imaginary Blenkensops?"

"They're not Blenkensops. Blenkensop was my second husband. My first husband's name was Hill. There are three pages of Hills in the telephone book. You couldn't check up on all the Hills if you tried."

Tommy sighed.

"It's the old trouble with you, Tuppence. You *will* overdo things. Two husbands and three sons. It's too much. You'll contradict yourself over the details."

"No, I shan't. And I rather fancy the sons may come in useful. I'm not under orders, remember. I'm a free-lance. I'm in this to enjoy myself and I'm going to enjoy myself."

"So it seems," said Tommy. He added gloomily: "If you ask me, the whole thing's a farce."

"Why do you say that?"

"Well, you've been at Sans Souci longer than I have. Can you honestly say you think any one of those people who were there last night could be a dangerous enemy agent?"

Tuppence said thoughtfully:

"It does seem a little incredible. There's the young man, of course."

"Carl von Deinim? The police check up on refugees, don't they?"

"I suppose so. Still, it might be managed. He's an attractive young man, you know."

"Meaning the girls will tell him things? But what girls? No Generals' or Admirals' daughters floating around here. Perhaps he walks out with a Company Commander in the A.T.S."

"Be quiet, Tommy. We ought to be taking this seriously."

"I am taking it seriously. It's just that I feel we're on a wild goose chase."

Tuppence said seriously:

"It's too early to say that. After all, nothing's going to be obvious about this business. What about Mrs. Perenna?"

"Yes," said Tommy thoughtfully, "there's Mrs. Perenna, I admit—she does want explaining."

Tuppence said in a business-like tone:

"What about us? I mean, how are we going to co-operate?"

Tommy said thoughtfully:

"We mustn't be seen about too much together."

"No, it would be fatal to suggest we know each other better than we appear to do. What we want to decide is the attitude. I think—yes, I think—pursuit is the best angle."

"Pursuit?"

"Exactly. I pursue you. You do your best to escape, but being a mere chivalrous male doesn't always succeed. I've had two husbands and I'm on the look-out for a third. You act the part of the hunted widower. Every now and then I pin you down somewhere, pen you in a café, catch you walking on the front. Everyone sniggers and thinks it very funny."

"Sounds feasible," agreed Tommy.

Tuppence said: "There's a kind of age-long humour about the chased male. That ought to stand us in good stead. If we are seen together, all anyone will do is to snigger and say, 'Look at poor old Meadowes.'"

Tommy gripped her arm suddenly.

"Look," he said. "Look ahead of you."

By the corner of one of the shelters a young man stood talking to a girl. They were both very earnest, very wrapped up in what they were saying.

Tuppence said softly:

"Carl von Deinim. Who's the girl, I wonder?"

"She's remarkably good looking, whoever she is."

Tuppence nodded. Her eyes dwelt thoughtfully on the dark passionate face, and on the tight-fitting pullover that revealed the lines of the girl's figure. She was talking earnestly, with emphasis. Carl von Deinim was listening to her.

Tuppence murmured:

"I think this is where you leave me."

"Right," agreed Tommy.

He turned and strolled in the opposite direction.

At the end of the promenade he encountered Major Bletchley. The latter peered at him suspiciously and then grunted out, "Good morning."

"Good morning."

"See you're like me, an early riser," remarked Bletchley.

Tommy said:

"One gets in the habit of it out East. Of course, that's many years ago now, but I still wake early."

"Quite right, too," said Major Bletchley with approval. "God, these young fellows nowadays make me sick. Hot baths—coming down to breakfast at ten o'clock or later. No wonder the Germans have been putting it over on us. No stamina. Soft lot of young pups. Army's not what it was, anyway. Coddle 'em, that's what they do nowadays. Tuck 'em up at night with hot water bottles. Faugh! Makes me sick!"

Tommy shook his head in a melancholy fashion and Major Bletchley, thus encouraged, went on.

"Discipline, that's what we need. Discipline. How are we going to win the War without discipline? Do you know, sir, some of these fellows come on parade in slacks—so I've been told. Can't expect to win a War that way. Slacks! My God!"

Mr. Meadowes hazarded the opinion that things were very different from what they had been.

"It's all this democracy," said Major Bletchley gloomily. "You can overdo anything. In my opinion they're overdoing the democracy business. Mixing up the officers and the men, feeding together in restaurants—Paugh!—the men don't like it, Meadowes. The troops know. The troops always know."

"Of course," said Mr. Meadowes, "I have no real knowledge of Army matters myself—"

The Major interrupted him, shooting a quick sideways glance.

"In the show in the last War?"

"Oh, yes."

"Thought so. Saw you'd been drilled. Shoulders. What regiment?"

"Fifth Corfeshires." Tommy remembered to produce Meadowes' military record.

"Ah, yes, Salonica!"

"Yes."

"I was in Mespot."

Bletchley plunged into reminiscences. Tommy listened politely. Bletchley ended up wrathfully.

"And will they make use of me now? No, they will not. Too old. Too old be damned. I could teach one or two of these young cubs something about war."

"Even if it's only what not to do?" suggested Tommy with a smile.

"Eh, what's that?"

A sense of humour was clearly not Major Bletchley's strong suit. He peered suspiciously at his companion. Tommy hastened to change the conversation.

"Know anything about that Mrs.—Blenkensop, I think her name is?"

"That's right. Blenkensop. Not a bad looking woman—bit long in the tooth—talks too much. Nice woman, but foolish. No, I don't know her. She's only been at Sans Souci a couple of days." He added: "Why do you ask?"

Tommy explained.

"Happened to meet her just now. Wondered if she was always out as early as this?"

"Don't know, I'm sure. Women aren't usually given to walking before breakfast—thank God," he added.

"Amen," said Tommy. He went on: "I'm not much good at making polite conversation before breakfast. Hope I wasn't rude to the woman, but I wanted my exercise."

Major Bletchley displayed instant sympathy.

"I'm with you, Meadowes. I'm with you. Women are all very well in their place, but not before breakfast." He chuckled a little. "Better be careful, old man. She's a widow, you know."

"Is she?"

The Major dug him cheerfully in the ribs.

"*We* know what widows are. She's buried two husbands and if you ask me, she's on the look-out for number three. Keep a very wary eye open, Meadowes. A wary eye. That's my advice."

And in high good humour Major Bletchley wheeled about at the end of the parade and set the pace for a smart walk back to breakfast at Sans Souci.

In the meantime, Tuppence had gently continued her walk along the esplanade, passing quite close to the shelter and the young couple talking there. As she passed she caught a few words. It was the girl speaking.

"But you must be careful, Carl. The very least suspicion—"

Tuppence was out of earshot. Suggestive words? Yes, but capable of any number of harmless interpretations. Unobtrusively she turned and again passed the two. Again words floated to her.

"Smug, destestable English . . ."

The eyebrows of Mrs. Blenkensop rose ever so slightly.

Hardly, she thought, a very wise conversation. Carl von Deinim was a refugee from Nazi persecution, given asylum and shelter by England. Neither wise nor grateful to listen assentingly to such words.

Again Tuppence turned. But this time, before she reached the shelter, the couple had parted abruptly, the girl to cross the road leaving the sea front, Carl von Deinim to come along in Tuppence's direction.

He would not, perhaps, have recognized her but for her own pause and hesitation. Then quickly, he brought his heels together and bowed.

Tuppence twittered at him.

"Good morning, Mr. von Deinim, isn't it? Such a lovely morning."

"Ah, yes. The weather is fine."

Tuppence ran on.

"It quite tempted me. I don't often come out before breakfast. But this morning, what with not sleeping very well—one often doesn't sleep well in a strange place, I find. It takes a day or two to accustom oneself, I always say."

"Oh, yes, no doubt that is so."

"And really this little walk has quite given me an appetite for breakfast."

"You go back to Sans Souci now? If you permit I will walk with you." He walked gravely by her side.

Tuppence said:

"You also are out to get an appetite?"

Gravely he shook his head.

"Oh, no. My breakfast I have already had it. I am on my way to work."

"Work?"

"I am a research chemist."

So that's what you are, thought Tuppence, stealing a quick glance at him.

Carl von Deinim went on, his voice stiff.

"I came to this country to escape Nazi persecution. I had very little money—no friends. I do now what useful work I can."

He stared straight ahead of him. Tuppence was conscious of some undercurrent of strong feeling moving him powerfully.

She murmured vaguely:

"Oh, yes, I see. I see. Very creditable, I am sure."

Carl von Deinim said:

"My two brothers are in concentration camps. My father died in one. My mother died of sorrow and fear."

Tuppence thought:

"The way he says that—as though he had learned it by heart."

Again she stole a quick glance at him. He was still staring ahead of him, his face impassive.

They walked in silence for some moments. Two men passed them. One of them shot a quick glance at Carl. She heard him mutter to his companion:

"Bet you that fellow is a German."

Tuppence saw the colour rise in Carl von Deinim's cheeks. Suddenly he lost command of himself. That tide of hidden emotion came to the surface. He stammered:

"You heard—you heard—that is what they say—I—"

"My dear boy!" Tuppence reverted suddenly to her real self. Her voice was crisp and compelling. "Don't be an idiot. You can't have it both ways."

He turned his head and stared at her.

"What do you mean?"

"You're a refugee. You have to take the rough with the smooth. You're alive, that's the main thing. Alive and free. For the other—realize that it's inevitable. This country's at War. You're a German." She smiled suddenly. "You can't expect the mere man in the street—literally the man in the street—to distinguish between bad Germans and good Germans, if I may put it so crudely."

He still stared at her. His eyes, so very blue, were poignant with suppressed feeling. Then, suddenly, he too smiled. He said:

"They said of Red Indians, did they not, that a good Indian was a dead Indian?" He laughed. "To be a good German I must be on time at my work. Please. Good morning."

Again that stiff bow. Tuppence stared after his retreating figure. She said to herself:

"Mrs. Blenkensop, you had a lapse then. Strict attention to business in future. Now for breakfast at Sans Souci."

The hall door of Sans Souci was open. Inside, Mrs. Perenna was conducting a vigorous conversation with someone.

"And you'll tell him what I think of that last lot of margarine. Get the cooked ham at Quiller's—it was twopence cheaper last time there, and be careful about the cabbages—"

She broke off as Tuppence entered.

"Oh, good morning, Mrs. Blenkensop, you are an early bird. You haven't had breakfast yet. It's all ready in the dining room." She added, indicating her companion: "My daughter, Sheila. You haven't met her. She's been away and only came home last night."

Tuppence looked with interest at the vivid, handsome face. No longer full of tragic energy, bored now, and resentful. "My daughter Sheila. Sheila Perenna."

Tuppence murmured a few pleasant words and went into the dining room. There were three people breakfasting—Mrs. Sprot and her baby girl, and big Mrs. O'Rourke. Tuppence said, "Good morning" and Mrs. O'Rourke replied with a hearty, "The top of the morning to you" that quite drowned Mrs. Sprot's more anaemic salutation.

The old woman started at Tuppence with a kind of devouring interest.

" 'Tis a fine thing to be out walking before breakfast," she observed. "A grand appetite it gives you."

Mrs. Sprot said to her offspring:

"*Nice* bread and milk, darling," and endeavoured to insinuate a spoonful into Miss Betty Sprot's mouth.

The latter cleverly circumvented this endeavour by an adroit movement of her head, and continued to stare at Tuppence with large round eyes.

She pointed a milky finger at the newcomer, gave her a dazzling smile and observed in gurgling tones: "Ga—Ga Bouch."

"She likes you," cried Mrs. Sprot, beaming on Tuppence as on one marked out for favour. "Sometimes she's so shy with strangers."

"Bouch," said Betty Sprot. "Ah pooth ah bag," she added with emphasis.

"And what would she be meaning by that?" demanded Mrs. O'Rourke, with interest.

"She doesn't speak awfully clearly yet," confessed Mrs. Sprot. "She's only just over two, you know. I'm afraid most of what she says is just Bosh. She can say Mama, though, can't you, darling?"

Betty looked thoughtfully at her mother and remarked with an air of finality:

"Guggle bick."

" 'Tis a language of their own they have, the little angels," boomed out Mrs. O'Rourke. "Betty darling, say Mama now."

Betty looked hard at Mrs. O'Rourke, frowned and observed with terrific emphasis: "Nazer—"

"There now, if she isn't doing her best! And a lovely sweet girl she is."

Mrs. O'Rourke rose, beamed in a ferocious manner at Betty, and waddled heavily out of the room.

"Ga, ga ga," said Betty with enormous satisfaction, and beat with a spoon on the table.

Tuppence said with a twinkle:

"What does Na-zer really mean?"

Mrs. Sprot said with a flush: "I'm afraid, you know, it's what Betty says when she doesn't like anyone or anything."

"I rather thought so," said Tuppence.

Both women laughed.

"After all," said Mrs. Sprot, "Mrs. O'Rourke means to be kind but she is rather alarming—with that deep voice and the beard and—and everything."

With her head on one side Betty made a cooing noise at Tuppence.

"She has taken to you, Mrs. Blenkensop," said Mrs. Sprot.

There was a slight jealous chill, Tuppence fancied, in her voice. Tuppence hastened to adjust matters.

"They always like a new face, don't they?" she said easily.

The door opened and Major Bletchley and Tommy appeared. Tuppence became arch.

"Ah, Mr. Meadowes," she called out. "I've beaten you, you see. First past the post. But I've left you just a *little* breakfast!"

She indicated with the faintest of gestures the seat beside her.

Tommy, muttering vaguely: "Oh, er—rather—thanks," and hurriedly sat down at the other end of the table.

Betty Sprot said *"Putch!"* with a fine splutter of milk at Major Bletchley, whose face instantly assumed a sheepish but delighted expression.

"And how's little Miss Bo Peep this morning?" he asked fatuously. "Bo Peep!" He enacted the play with a newspaper.

Betty crowed with delight.

Serious misgivings shook Tuppence. She thought:

"There *must* be some mistake. There *can't* be anything going on here. There simply can't!"

To believe in Sans Souci as a headquarters of the Fifth Column needed the mental equipment of the White Queen in *Alice.*

3

On the sheltered terrace outside, Miss Minton was knitting.

Miss Minton was thin and angular, her neck was stringy. She wore pale sky-blue jumpers, and chains or bead necklaces. Her skirts were tweedy and had a depressed droop at the back. She greeted Tuppence with alacrity.

"Good morning, Mrs. Blenkensop. I do hope you slept well."

Mrs. Blenkensop confessed that she never slept very well the first night or two in a strange bed. Miss Minton said, "Now wasn't that curious? It was exactly the same with *me*."

Mrs. Blenkensop said, "What a coincidence, and what a very pretty stitch that was." Miss Minton, flushing with pleasure, displayed it. "Yes, it was rather uncommon, and really quite simple. She could easily show it to Mrs. Blenkensop if Mrs. Blenkensop liked." "Oh, that was very kind of Miss Minton, but Mrs. Blenkensop was so stupid, she wasn't really very good at knitting, not at following patterns, that was to say. She could only do simple things like Balaclava helmets, and even now she was afraid she had gone wrong somewhere. It didn't look *right*, somehow, did it?"

Miss Minton cast an expert eye over the khaki mass. Gently she pointed out just what had gone wrong. Thankfully, Tuppence handed the faulty helmet over. Miss Minton exuded kindness and patronage. "Oh, no, it wasn't a trouble at all. She had knitted for so many years."

"I'm afraid I've never done any before this dreadful

War," confessed Tuppence. "But one feels so terribly, doesn't one, that one must do *something*."

"Oh, yes, indeed. And you actually have a boy in the Navy, I think I heard you say last night?"

"Yes, my eldest boy. Such a splendid boy he is—though I suppose a mother shouldn't say so. Then I have a boy in the Air Force and Cyril, my baby, is out in France."

"Oh, dear, dear, how terribly anxious you must be."

Tuppence thought:

"Oh, Derek, my darling Derek. . . . Out in the hell and mess—and here I am playing the fool—acting the thing I'm really feeling . . ."

She said in her most righteous voice:

"We must all be brave, mustn't we? Let's hope it will all be over soon. I was told the other day on very high authority indeed that the Germans can't possibly last out more than another two months."

Miss Minton nodded with so much vigour that all her bead chains rattled and shook.

"Yes, indeed, and I believe"—her voice lowered mysteriously—"that Hitler is suffering from a *disease*—absolutely fatal—he'll be raving mad by August."

Tuppence replied briskly:

"All this Blitzkrieg is just the Germans' last effort. I believe the shortage is something frightful in Germany. The men in the factories are very dissatisfied. The whole thing will crack up."

"What's this? What's all this?"

Mr. and Mrs. Cayley came out on the terrace, Mr. Cayley putting his questions fretfully. He settled himself in a chair and his wife put a rug over his knees. He repeated fretfully:

"What's that you are saying?"

"We're saying," said Miss Minton, "that it will all be over by the Autumn."

"Nonsense," said Mr. Cayley. "This War is going to last at least six years."

"Oh, Mr. Cayley," protested Tuppence. "You don't really think so?"

Mr. Cayley was peering about him suspiciously.

"Now I wonder," he murmured. "Is there a draught?

Perhaps it would be better if I moved my chair back into the corner."

The resettlement of Mr. Cayley took place. His wife, an anxious-faced woman who seemed to have no other aim in life than to minister to Mr. Cayley's wants, manipulating cushions and rugs, asking from time to time: "Now, how is that, Alfred? Do you think that will be all right? Ought you, perhaps, to have your sun glasses? There is rather a glare this morning."

Mr. Cayley said irritably:

"No, no. Don't fuss, Elisabeth. Have you got my muffler? No, no, my silk muffler. Oh, well, it doesn't matter. I daresay this will do—for once. But I don't want to get my throat overheated, and wool—in this sunlight—well, perhaps you *had* better fetch the other." He turned his attention back to matters of public interest. "Yes," he said. "I give it six years."

He listened with pleasure to the protests of the two women.

"You dear ladies are just indulging in what we call wishful thinking. Now I know Germany. I may say I know Germany extremely well. In the course of my business before I retired I used to be constantly to and fro. Berlin, Hamburg, Munich, I know them all. I can assure you that Germany can hold out practically indefinitely. With Russia behind her—"

Mr. Cayley plunged triumphantly on, his voice rising and falling in pleasurably melancholy cadences, only interrupted when he paused to receive the silk muffler his wife brought him and wind it round his throat.

Mrs. Sprot brought out Betty and plumped her down with a small woolen dog that lacked an ear and a woolly doll's jacket.

"There, Betty," she said. "You dress up Bonzo ready for his walk while Mummy gets ready to go out."

Mr. Cayley's voice droned on, reciting statistics and figures, all of a depressing character. The monologue was punctuated by a cheerful twittering from Betty talking busily to Bonzo in her own language.

"Truckle—truckly—pah bat," said Betty. Then, as a bird

alighted near her, she stretched out loving hands to it and gurgled. The bird flew away and Betty glanced round the assembled company and remarked clearly:

"Dicky," and nodded her head with great satisfaction.

"That child is learning to talk in the most wonderful way," said Miss Minton. "Say Ta ta, Betty. Ta ta."

Betty looked at her coldly and remarked:

"Gluck!"

Then she forced Bonzo's one arm into his woolly coat and, toddling over to a chair, picked up the cushion and pushed Bonzo behind it. Chuckling gleefully, she said with terrific pains:

"Hide! Bow wow. Hide."

Miss Minton, acting as a kind of interpreter, said with vicarious pride:

"She loves hide and seek. She's always hiding things." She cried out with exaggerated surprise:

"*Where* is Bonzo? Where *is* Bonzo? Where *can* Bonzo have gone?"

Betty flung herself down and went into ecstasies of mirth.

Mr. Cayley, finding attention diverted from his explanation of Germany's methods of substitution of raw materials, looked put out and coughed aggressively.

Mrs. Sprot came out with her hat on and picked up Betty. Attention returned to Mr. Cayley.

"You were saying, Mr. Cayley?" said Tuppence.

But Mr. Cayley was affronted. He said coldly:

"That woman is always plumping that child down and expecting people to look after it. I think I'll have the woollen muffler after all, dear. The sun is going in."

"Oh, but, Mr. Cayley, do go on with what you were telling us. It was so interesting," Miss Minton begged.

Mollified, Mr. Cayley weightily resumed his discourse, drawing the folds of the woolly muffler closer round his stringy neck.

"As I was saying, Germany has so perfected her system of—"

Tuppence turned to Mrs. Cayley, and asked:

"What do you think about the war, Mrs. Cayley?"

Mrs. Cayley jumped.

"Oh, what do I think? What—what do you mean?"

"Do you think it will last as long as six years?"

Mrs. Cayley said doubtfully:

"Oh, I hope not. It's a very long time, isn't it?"

"Yes, a long time. What do you really think?"

Mrs. Cayley seemed quite alarmed by the question. She said:

"Oh, I—I don't know. I don't know at all. Alfred says it will."

"But you don't think so?"

"Oh, I don't know. It's difficult to say, isn't it?"

Tuppence felt a wave of exasperation. The chirruping Miss Minton, the dictatorial Mr. Cayley, the nitwitted Mrs. Cayley—were these people really typical of her fellow countrymen? Was Mrs. Sprot any better with her slightly vacant face and the boiled gooseberry eyes? What could she, Tuppence, ever find out here? Not one of these people, surely—

Her thought was checked. She was aware of a shadow. Someone behind her who stood between her and the sun. She turned her head.

Mrs. Perenna, standing on the terrace, her eyes on the group. And something in those eyes—scorn, was it? A kind of withering contempt. Tuppence thought:

I must find out more about Mrs. Perenna.

TWO

Tommy was establishing the happiest of relationships with Major Bletchley.

"Brought down some golf clubs with you, didn't you Meadowes?"

Tommy pleaded guilty.

"Ha! I can tell you, *my* eyes don't miss much. Splendid! We must have a game together. Ever play on the links here?"

Tommy replied in the negative.

"They're not bad—not bad at all. Bit on the short side, perhaps, but lovely view over the sea and all that. And never very crowded. Look here, what about coming along with me this morning? We might have a game."

"Thanks very much. I'd like it."

"Must say I'm glad you've arrived," remarked Bletchley as they were trudging up the hill. "Too many women in that place. Gets on one's nerves. Glad I've got another fellow to keep me in countenance. You can't count Cayley—the man's a kind of walking chemist's shop. Talks of nothing but his health and the treatments he's tried and the drugs he's taking. If he threw away all his little pill boxes and went out for a good ten mile walk every day he'd be a different man. The only other male in the place is von Deinim, and to tell you the truth, Meadowes, I'm not too easy in my mind about him."

"No?" said Tommy.

"No. You take my word for it, this refugee business is dangerous. If I had my way I'd intern the lot of them. Safety first."

"A bit drastic, perhaps."

"Not at all. War's War. And I've got my suspicions of Master Carl. For one thing, he's clearly not a Jew. Then he came over here just a month—only a month, mind you—before War broke out. That's a bit suspicious."

Tommy said invitingly:

"Then you think—"

"*Spying*—that's his little game!"

"But surely there's nothing of great military or naval importance hereabouts?"

"Ah, old man, that's where the artfulness comes in! If he were anywhere near Plymouth or Portsmouth he'd be under supervision. In a sleepy place like this, nobody bothers. But it's on the coast, isn't it? The truth of it is the Government is a great deal too easy with these enemy aliens. Anyone who cared could come over here and pull a long face and talk about their brothers in concentration camps. Look at that young man—arrogance in every line of him. He's a Nazi—that's what he is—a Nazi."

"What we really need in this country is a witch doctor or two," said Tommy pleasantly.

"Eh, what's that?"

"To smell out the spies," Tommy explained gravely.

"Ha, very good that—very good. Smell 'em out—yes, of course."

Further conversation was brought to an end, for they had arrived at the clubhouse.

Tommy's name was put down as a temporary member, he was introduced to the secretary, a vacant looking elderly man, and with the subscription duly paid, Tommy and the Major started on their round.

Tommy was a mediocre golfer. He was glad to find that his standard of play was just about right for his new friend. The Major won by two up and one to play, a very happy state of events.

"Good match, Meadowes, very good match—you had bad luck with that mashie shot, just turned off at the last minute. We must have a game fairly often. Come along and I'll introduce you to some of the fellows. Nice lot on the whole; some of them inclined to be rather old women, if you know what I mean? Ah, here's Haydock—you'll like Haydock. Retired naval wallah. Has that house on the cliff next door to us. He's our local A.R.P. warden."

Commander Haydock was a big hearty man with a weatherbeaten face, intensely blue eyes, and a habit of shouting most of his remarks.

He greeted Tommy with friendliness.

"So you're going to keep Bletchley countenance at Sans Souci? He'll be glad of another man. Rather swamped by female society, eh, Bletchley?"

"I'm not much of a ladies' man," said Major Bletchley.

"Nonsense," said Haydock. "Not your type of lady, my boy, that's it. Old boarding house pussies. Nothing to do but gossip and knit."

"You're forgetting Miss Perenna," said Bletchley.

"Ah, Sheila—she's an attractive girl all right. Regular beauty if you ask me."

"I'm a bit worried about her," said Bletchley.

"What do you mean? Have a drink, Meadowes? What's yours, Major?"

The drinks ordered and the men settled on the verandah of the clubhouse, Haydock repeated his question.

Major Bletchley said with some violence:

"That German chap. She's seeing too much of him."

"Getting sweet on him, you mean? H'm, that's bad. Of course he's a good looking young chap in his way. But it won't do. It won't do, Bletchley. We can't have that sort of thing. Trading with the enemy, that's what it amounts to. These girls—where's their proper spirit? Plenty of decent young English fellows about."

Bletchley said:

"Sheila's a queer girl—she gets odd sullen fits when she will hardly speak to anyone."

"Spanish blood," said the Commander. "Her father was half Spanish, wasn't he?"

"Don't know. It's a Spanish name, I should think."

The Commander glanced at his watch.

"About time for the news. We'd better go in and listen to it."

The news was meagre that day, little more in it than had been already in the morning papers. After commenting with approval on the latest exploits of the Air Force—first-rate chaps, brave as lions—the Commander went on to develop his own pet theory—that sooner or later the Germans would attempt a landing at Leahampton itself—his argument being that it was such an unimportant spot.

"Not even an anti-aircraft gun in the place! Disgraceful!"

The argument was not developed, for Tommy and the Major had to hurry back to lunch at Sans Souci. Haydock extended a cordial invitation to Tommy to come and see his little place, "Smugglers' Rest." "Marvellous view—my own beach—every kind of handy gadget in the house. Bring him along, Bletchley."

It was settled that Tommy and Major Bletchley should come in for drinks on the evening of the following day.

THREE

After lunch was a peaceful time at Sans Souci. Mr. Cayley went to have his "rest" with the devoted Mrs. Cayley in attendance. Mrs. Blenkensop was conducted by Miss Minton to a depot to pack and address parcels for the Front.

Mr. Meadowes strolled gently out into Leahampton and along the front. He bought a few cigarettes, stopped at Smith's to purchase the latest number of *Punch*, then after a few minutes of apparent irresolution, he entered a bus bearing the legend OLD PIER.

The old pier was at the extreme end of the promenade. That part of Leahampton was known to house agents as the least desirable end. It was West Leahampton and poorly thought of. Tommy paid twopence and strolled up the pier. It was a flimsy and weather-worn affair with a few moribund penny-in-the-slot machines placed at far distant intervals. There was no one on it but some children running up and down and screaming in voices that matched quite accurately the screaming of the gulls, and one solitary man sitting on the end fishing.

Mr. Meadowes strolled up to the end and gazed down into the water. Then he asked gently:

"Caught anything?"

The fisherman shook his head.

"Don't often get a bite." Mr. Grant reeled in his line a bit. He said without turning his head:

"What about you, Meadowes?"

Tommy said:

"Nothing much to report as yet, sir. I'm digging myself in."

"Good. Tell me."

Tommy sat on an adjacent post, so placed that he commanded the length of the pier. Then he began.

"I've gone down quite all right, I think. I gather you've already got a list of the people there?" Grant nodded. "There's nothing much to report as yet. I've struck up a friendship with Major Bletchley. We played golf this morning. He seems the ordinary type of retired officer. If anything, a shade too typical. Cayley seems a genuine hypochondriacal invalid. That, again, would be an easy part to act. He has, by his own admission, been a good deal in Germany during the last few years.

"A point," said Grant, laconically.

"Then there's von Deinim."

"Yes. I don't need to tell you, Meadowes, that von

Deinim's the one I'm most interested in."

"You think he's N?"

Grant shook his head.

"No, I don't. As I see it, N couldn't afford to be a German."

"Not a refugee from Nazi persecution, even?"

"Not even that. We watch, and they know we watch, all the enemy aliens in this country. Moreover—this is in confidence, Beresford—very shortly all enemy aliens between 16 and 60 will be interned. Whether our adversaries are aware of the fact or not, they can at any rate anticipate that such a thing might happen. They would never risk the head of their organization being interned. N, therefore, must be either a neutral—or else he is (apparently) an Englishman. The same, of course, applies to M. No, my meaning about von Deinim is this: He may be a link in the chain. N or M may not be at Sans Souci, it may be Carl von Deinim who is there and through him we may be led to our objective. That does seem to be highly possible. The more so as I cannot very well see that any of the other inmates of Sans Souci are likely to be the person we are seeking."

"You've had them more or less investigated, I suppose, sir?"

Grant sighed—a sharp quick sigh of vexation.

"No, that's just what it's impossible for me to do. I could have them looked up by the department easily enough—*but I can't risk it, Beresford*. For, you see, the rot is in the department itself. One hint that I've got my eye on Sans Souci for any reason—and the organization may be put wise. That's where *you* come in, the outsider. That's why you've got to work in the dark, without help from us. It's our only chance—and I daren't risk alarming them. There's only one person I've been able to check up on."

"Who's that, sir?"

Grant smiled.

"Carl von Deinim himself. That's easy enough. Routine. I can have him looked up—not from the Sans Souci angle, but from the enemy alien angle."

Tommy asked curiously:

"And the result?"

A curious smile came over the other's face.

"Master Carl is exactly what he says he is. His father was indiscreet, was arrested and died in a concentration camp. Carl's elder brothers are in camps. His mother died in great distress of mind a year ago. He escaped to England a month before war broke out. Von Deinim has professed himself anxious to help this country. His work in a chemical research laboratory has been excellent and most helpful on the problem of immunizing certain gases and in general decontamination experiments."

Tommy said:

"Then he's all right?"

"Not necessarily. Our German friends are notorious for their thoroughness. If von Deinim was sent as an agent to England special care would be taken that his record should be consistent with his own account of himself. There are two possibilities. The whole von Deinim family may be parties to the arrangement—not improbable under the painstaking Nazi régime. Or else this is not really Carl von Deinim but *a man playing the part of Carl von Deinim.*"

Tommy said slowly: "I see." He added inconsequently:

"He seems an awfully nice young fellow."

Sighing, Grant said: "They are—they nearly always are. It's an odd life this service of ours. We respect our adversaries and they respect us. You usually like your opposite number, you know—even when you're doing your best to down him."

There was a silence as Tommy thought over the strange anomaly of war. Grant's voice broke into his musings.

"But there are those for whom we've neither respect nor liking—and those are the traitors within our own ranks—the men who are willing to betray their country and accept office and promotion from the foreigner who has conquered it."

Tommy said with feeling:

"My God, I'm with you, sir. That's a skunk's trick."

"And deserves a skunk's end."

Tommy said incredulously:

"And there really are these—these swine?"

"Everywhere. As I told you. In our service. In the fighting

forces. On Parliamentary benches. High up in the Ministries. We've got to comb them out—we've *got* to! And we must do it quickly. It can't be done from the bottom—the small fry, the people who speak in the Parks, who sell their wretched little news-sheets, they don't know who the big bugs are. It's the big bugs we want, they're the people who can do untold damage—and will do it unless we're in time."

Tommy said confidently:

"We shall be in time, sir."

Grant asked:

"What makes you say that?"

Tommy said:

"You've just said it—we've *got* to be!"

The man with the fishing line turned and looked full at his subordinate for a minute or two, taking in anew the quiet resolute line of the jaw. He had a new liking and appreciation of what he saw. He said quietly:

"Good man."

He went on:

"What about the women in this place? Anything strike you as suspicious there?"

"I think there's something odd about the woman who runs it."

"Mrs. Perenna?"

"Yes. You don't—know anything about her?"

Grant said slowly:

"I might see what I could do about checking her antecedents, but as I told you, it's risky."

"Yes, better not take any chances. She's the only one who strikes me as suspicious in any way. There's a young mother, a fussy spinster, the hypochondriac's brainless wife, and a rather fearsome looking old Irishwoman. All seem harmless enough on the face of it."

"That's the lot, is it?"

"No. There's a Mrs. Blenkensop—arrived three days ago."

"Well?"

Tommy said:

"Mrs. Blenkensop is my wife."

"*What?*"

In the surprise of the announcement Grant's voice was

raised. He spun around, sharp anger in his gaze. "I thought I told you, Beresford, not to breathe a word to your wife!"

"Quite right, sir, and I didn't. If you'll just listen——"

Succinctly, Tommy narrated what had occurred. He did not dare look at the other. He carefully kept out of his voice the pride that he secretly felt.

There was a silence when he brought the story to an end. Then a queer noise escaped from the other. Grant was laughing. He laughed for some minutes.

He said:

"I take my hat off to the woman! She's one in a thousand!"

"I agree," said Tommy.

"Easthampton will laugh when I tell him this. He warned me not to leave her out. Said she'd get the better of me if I did. I wouldn't listen to him. It shows you, though, how damned careful you've got to be. I thought I'd taken every precaution against being overheard. I'd satisfied myself beforehand that you and your wife were alone in the flat. I actually heard the voice in the telephone asking your wife to come round at once, and so—and so I was tricked by the old simple device of the banged door. Yes, she's a smart woman, your wife."

He was silent for a minute, then he said:

"Tell her from me, will you, that I eat dirt?"

"And I suppose, now, she's in on this?"

Mr. Grant made an expressive grimace.

"She's in on it whether we like it or not. Tell her the department will esteem it an honour if she will condescend to work with us over the matter."

"I'll tell her," said Tommy with a faint grin.

Grant said seriously:

"You couldn't persuade her, I suppose, to go home and stay home?"

Tommy shook his head.

"You don't know Tuppence."

"I think I am beginning to. I said that because—well, it's a very dangerous business. If they get wise to you or to her——"

He left the sentence unfinished.

Tommy said gravely:

"I do understand that, sir."

"But I suppose even you couldn't persuade your wife to keep out of danger."

Tommy said slowly:

"I don't know that I really would want to do that . . . Tuppence and I, you see, aren't on those terms. We go into things—together!"

In his mind was that phrase, uttered years ago, at the close of an earlier war. A *joint venture*. . . .

That was what his life with Tuppence had been and would always be—a Joint Venture. . . .

4

When Tuppence entered the lounge at Sans Souci just before dinner, the only occupant of the room was the monumental Mrs. O'Rourke, who was sitting by the window looking like some gigantic Buddha.

She greeted Tuppence with a lot of geniality and verve.

"Ah, now, if it isn't Mrs. Blenkensop! You're like myself, it pleases you to be down on time and get a quiet minute or two here before going into the dining room, and a pleasant room this is in good weather with the windows open in the way that you'll not be noticing the smell of cooking. Terrible that is, in all of these places, and more especially if it's onion or cabbage that's on the fire. Sit here now, Mrs. Blenkensop, and tell me what you've been doing with yourself this fine day and how do you like Leahampton."

There was something about Mrs. O'Rourke that had an unholy fascination for Tuppence. She was rather like an ogress dimly remembered from early fairy tales. With her bulk, her deep voice, her unabashed beard and moustache, her deep twinkling eyes and the impression she gave of being more than life-size, she was indeed not unlike some childhood fantasy.

Tuppence replied that she thought she was going to like Leahampton very much, and be happy there.

"That is," she added in a melancholy voice, "as happy as I can be anywhere with this terrible anxiety weighing on me all the time."

"Ah, now, don't you be worrying yourself," Mrs. O'Rourke advised comfortably. "Those fine boys of yours

will come back to you safe and sound. Not a doubt of it.
One of them's in the Air Force, so I think you said?"

"Yes, Raymond."

"And is he in France now, or in England?"

"He's in Egypt at the moment, but from what he said in
his last letter—not exactly *said*—but we have a little private
code if you know what I mean?—certain sentences mean
certain things. I think that's quite justified, don't you?"

Mrs. O'Rourke replied promptly:

"Indeed and I do. 'Tis a mother's privilege."

"Yes, you see I feel I must know just where he is."

Mrs. O'Rourke nodded the Buddha-like head.

"I feel for you entirely, so I do. If I had a boy out there
I'd be deceiving the censor the very same way, so I would.
And your other boy, the one in the Navy?"

Tuppence entered obligingly upon a saga of Douglas.

"You see," she ended. "I feel so lost without my three
boys. They've never been all away together from me before.
They're all so sweet to me. I really do think they treat me
more as a *friend* than a mother." She laughed self-con-
sciously. "I have to scold them sometimes and *make* them
go out without me."

("What a pestilential woman I sound," thought Tuppence
to herself.)

She went on aloud.

"And really I didn't know quite *what* to do or *where* to
go. The lease of my house in London was up and it seemed
so foolish to renew it and I thought if I came somewhere
quiet, and yet with a good train service—" She broke off.

Again the Buddha nodded.

"I agree with you entirely. London is no place at the
present. Ah! the gloom of it! I've lived there myself for
many a year now. I'm by way of being an antique dealer,
you know. You may know my shop in Cornaby Street,
Chelsea? Kate Kelly's the name over the door. Lovely stuff
I had there, too—oh, lovely stuff—mostly glass—Waterford,
Cork—beautiful Chandeliers and lustres and punchbowls
and all the rest of it. Foreign glass too. And small furniture—nothing large—just small period pieces—mostly wal-
nut and oak. Oh, lovely stuff—and I had some good cus-

tomers. But there, when there's a War on, all that goes west. I'm lucky to be out of it with as little loss as I've had."

A faint memory flickered through Tuppence's mind. A shop filled with glass, through which it was difficult to move, a rich persuasive voice, a compelling massive woman. Yes, surely, she had been into that shop.

Mrs. O'Rourke went on.

"I'm not one of those that like to be always complaining —not like some that's in this house. Mr. Cayley for one, with his muffler and his shawls and his moans about his business going to pieces. Of course it's to pieces, there's a War on—and his wife with never Boo to say to a goose. Then there's that little Mrs. Sprot, always fussing about her husband."

"Is he out at the front?"

"Not he. He's a tuppenny-halfpenny clerk in an insurance office, that's all, and so terrified of air raids he's had his wife down here since the beginning of the War. Mind you, I think that's right where the child's concerned—and a nice wee mite she is—but Mrs. Sprot, she frets, for all that her husband comes down when he can. . . . Keeps saying Arthur must miss her so. But if you ask me Arthur's not missing her overmuch—maybe he's got other fish to fry."

Tuppence murmured:

"I'm terribly sorry for all these mothers. If you let your children go away without you, you never stop worrying. And if you go with them it's hard on the husbands being left."

"Ah! yes, and it comes expensive running two establishments."

"This place seems quite reasonable," said Tuppence.

"Yes, I'd say you get your money's worth. Mrs. Perenna's a good manager. There's a queer woman for you now."

"In what way?" asked Tuppence.

Mrs. O'Rourke said with a twinkle:

"You'll be thinking I'm a terrible talker. It's true. I'm interested in all my fellow creatures, that's why I sit in this chair as often as I can. You see who goes in and who goes out and who's on the verandah and what goes on in the garden. What were we talking of now—ah, yes, Mrs. Per-

enna, and the queerness of her. There's been a grand drama
in that woman's life or I'm much mistaken."

"Do you really think so?"

"I do now. And the mystery she makes of herself! 'And
where might you come from in Ireland?' I asked her. And
would you believe it, she held out on me, declaring she was
not from Ireland at all."

"You think she is Irish?"

"Of course she's Irish. I know my own countrywomen.
I could name you the county she comes from. But there!
'I'm English,' she says, 'and my husband was a Span-
iard'—"

Mrs. O'Rourke broke off abruptly as Mrs. Sprot came
in, closely followed by Tommy.

Tuppence immediately assumed a sprightly manner.

"Good evening, Mr. Meadowes. You look very brisk this
evening."

Tommy said:

"Plenty of exercise, that's the secret. A round of golf this
morning and a walk along the front this afternoon."

Millicent Sprot said:

"I took Baby down to the beach this afternoon. She
wanted to paddle but I really thought it was rather cold. I
was helping her build a castle and a dog ran off with my
knitting and pulled out yards of it. So annoying, and so
difficult picking up all the stitches again. I'm such a bad
knitter."

"You're getting along fine with that helmet, Mrs. Blenkensop," said Mrs. O'Rourke, sudenly turning her attention
to Tuppence. "You've been just racing along. I thought Miss
Minton said that you were an inexperienced knitter."

Tuppence flushed faintly. Mrs. O'Rourke's eyes were
sharp. With a slightly vexed air, Tuppence said:

"I have really done quite a lot of knitting. I told Miss
Minton so. But I think she likes teaching people."

Everybody laughed in agreement, and a few minutes
later the rest of the party came in and the gong was sounded.

The conversation during the meal turned on the absorbing
subject of spies. Well-known hoary chestnuts were retold.

The nun with the muscular arm; the clergyman descending from his parachute and using unclergymanlike language as he landed with a bump; the Austrian cook who secreted a wireless in her bedroom chimney; and all the things that had happened or nearly happened to aunts and second cousins of those present. That led easily to Fifth Column activities. To denunciations of the British Fascists, of the Communists, of the Peace Party, of conscientious objectors. It was a very normal conversation, of the kind that may be heard almost every day, nevertheless Tuppence watched keenly the faces and demeanour of the people as they talked, striving to catch some tell-tale expression or word. But there was nothing. Sheila Perenna alone took no part in the conversation, but that might be put down to her habitual taciturnity. She sat there, her dark rebellious face sullen and brooding.

Carl von Deinim was out tonight, so tongues could be quite unrestrained.

Sheila only spoke once towards the end of dinner.

Mrs. Sprot had just said in her thin fluting voice:

"Where I do think the Germans made such a mistake in the last war was to shoot Nurse Cavell. It turned everybody against them."

It was then that Sheila, flinging back her head, demanded in her fierce young voice: "Why shouldn't they shoot her? She was a spy, wasn't she?"

"Oh, no, not a spy."

"She helped English people to escape—in an enemy country. That's the same thing. Why shouldn't she be shot?"

"Oh, but shooting a woman—and a nurse."

Sheila got up.

"I think the Germans were quite right," she said.

She went out of the window into the garden.

Dessert, consisting of some under-ripe bananas and some tired oranges, had been on the table some time. Everyone rose and adjourned to the lounge for coffee.

Only Tommy unobtrusively betook himself to the garden. He found Sheila Perenna leaning over the terrace wall staring out at the sea. He came and stood beside her.

By her hurried, quick breathing he knew that something
had upset her badly. He offered her a cigarette, which she
accepted.

He said:

"Lovely night."

In a low intense voice the girl answered:

"It could be. . . ."

Tommy looked at her doubtfully. He felt, suddenly, the
attraction and the vitality of this girl. There was a tumultu-
ous life in her, a kind of compelling power. She was the kind
of girl, he thought, that a man might easily lose his head
over.

"If it weren't for the War, you mean?" he said.

"I don't mean that at all. I hate the War."

"So do we all."

"Not in the way I mean. I hate the cant about it, the
smugness—the horrible, horrible patriotism."

"Patriotism?" Tommy was startled.

"Yes, I hate patriotism, do you understand? All this
country, country, country! Betraying your country—dying
for your country—serving your country. Why should one's
country mean anything at all?"

Tommy said simply: "I don't know. It just does."

"Not to me! Oh, it would to you—you go abroad and
buy and sell in the British Empire and come back bronzed
and full of clichés, talking about the natives and calling for
Chota Pegs and all that sort of thing."

Tommy said gently:

"I'm not quite as bad as that, I hope, my dear."

"I'm exaggerating a little—but you know what I mean.
You believe in the British Empire—and—and—the stupidity
of dying for one's country."

"My country," said Tommy drily, "doesn't seem particularly anxious to allow me to die for it."

"Yes, but you *want* to. And it's stupid! *Nothing's* worth
dying for. It's all an *idea*—talk—froth—high-flown idiocy.
My country doesn't mean anything to me at all."

"Some day," said Tommy, "you'll be surprised to find
that it does."

"No. Never. I've suffered—I've seen—"

She broke off—then turned suddenly and impetuously upon him.

"Do you know who my father was?"

"No." Tommy's interest quickened.

"His name was Patrick Maguire. He—he was a follower of Casement in the last War. He was shot as a traitor! All for nothing! For an idea—he worked himself up with those other Irishmen. Why couldn't he just stay at home quietly and mind his own business? He's a martyr to some people and a traitor to others. I think he was just—*stupid!*"

Tommy could hear the note of pent-up rebellion coming out into the open. He said:

"So that's the shadow you've grown up with?"

"Shadow's right. Mother changed her name. We lived in Spain for some years. She always says that my father was half a Spaniard. We always tell lies wherever we go. We've been all over the Continent. Finally we came here and started this place. I think this is quite the most hateful thing we've done yet."

Tommy asked:

"How does you mother feel about—things?"

"You mean—about my father's death." Sheila was silent a moment frowning, puzzled. She said slowly: "I've never really known . . . she never talks about it. It's not easy to know what mother feels or thinks."

Tommy nodded his head thoughtfully.

Sheila said abruptly:

"I—I don't know why I've been telling you this. I got worked up. Where did it all start?"

"A discussion on Edith Cavell."

"Oh, yes—patriotism. I said I hated it."

"Aren't you forgetting Nurse Cavell's own words?"

"What words?"

"Before she died. Don't you know what she said?"

He repeated the words:

"Patriotism is not enough . . . I must have no hatred in my heart."

"Oh." She stood there stricken for a moment.

Then, turning quickly, she wheeled away into the shadow of the garden.

TWO

"So you see, Tuppence, it would all fit in."

Tuppence nodded thoughtfully. The beach around them was empty. She herself leaned against a breakwater, Tommy sat above her, on the breakwater itself, from which post he could see anyone who approached along the esplanade. Not that he expected to see anyone, having ascertained with a fair amount of accuracy where people would be this morning. In any case his rendezvous with Tuppence had borne all the signs of a casual meeting, pleasurable to the lady and slightly alarming to himself.

Tuppence said:

"Mrs. Perenna?"

"Yes. M, not N. She satisfies the requirements."

Tuppence nodded thoughtfully again.

"Yes. She's Irish—as spotted by Mrs. O'Rourke—won't admit the fact. Has done a good deal of coming and going on the continent. Changed her name to Perenna, came here and started this boarding house. A splendid bit of camouflage, full of innocuous bores. Her husband was shot as a traitor—she's got every incentive for running a Fifth Column show in this country. Yes, it fits. Is the girl in it, too, do you think?"

Tommy said finally:

"Definitely not. She'd never have told me all this otherwise. I—I feel a bit of a cad, you know."

Tuppence nodded with complete understanding.

"Yes, one does. In a way it's a foul job, this."

"But very necessary."

"Oh, of course."

Tommy said, flushing slightly:

"I don't like lying any better than you do—"

Tuppence interrupted him.

"I don't mind lying in the least. To be quite honest I get a lot of artistic pleasure out of my lies. What gets me down is those moments when one forgets to lie—the times when one is just oneself—and gets results that way that you couldn't have got any other." She paused and went on: "That's what happened to you last night—with the girl.

She responded to the *real* you—that's why you feel badly about it."

"I believe you're right, Tuppence."

"I know. Because I did the same thing myself—with the German boy."

Tommy said:

"What do you think about him?"

Tuppence said quickly:

"If you ask me, I don't think he's got anything to do with it."

"Grant thinks he has."

"Your Mr. Grant!" Tuppence's mood changed. She chuckled. "How I'd like to have seen his face when you told him about me."

"At any rate, he's made the *amende honorable*. You're definitely on the job."

Tuppence nodded, but she looked a trifle abstracted.

She said:

"Do you remember after the last War—when we were hunting down Mr. Brown? Do you remember what fun it was? How excited we were?"

Tommy agreed, his face lighting up.

"Rather!"

"Tommy—why isn't it the same now?"

He considered the question, his quiet ugly face grave. Then he said:

"I suppose it's really—a question of age."

Tuppence said sharply:

"You don't think—we're too old?"

"No, I'm sure we're not. It's only that—this time—it won't be *fun*. It's the same in other ways. This is the second War we've been in—and we feel quite different about this one."

"I know—we see the pity of it and the waste—and the horror. All the things we were too young to think about before."

"That's it. In the last war I was scared every now and then—and had some pretty close shaves, and went through hell once or twice, but there were good times, too."

Tuppence said:

"I suppose Derek feels like that?"

"Better not think about him, old thing," Tommy advised.

"You're right." Tuppence set her teeth. "We've got a job. We're going to *do* that job. Let's get on with it. Have we found what we're looking for in Mrs. Perenna?"

"We can at least say that she's strongly indicated. There's no one else, is there, Tuppence, that you've got your eye on?"

Tuppence considered.

"No, there isn't. The first thing I did when I arrived, of course, was to size them all up and assess, as it were, possibilities. Some of them seem quite impossible."

"Such as?"

"Well, Miss Minton, for instance, the 'compleat' British spinster, and Mrs. Sprot and her Betty, and the vacuous Mrs. Cayley."

"Yes, but nitwittishness can be assumed."

"Oh, quite, but the fussy spinster and the absorbed young mothers are parts that would be fatally easy to overdo—and these people are quite natural. Then, where Mrs. Sprot is concerned, there's the child."

"I suppose," said Tommy, "that even a secret agent might have a child."

"Not with her on the job," said Tuppence. "It's not the kind of thing you'd bring a child into. I'm quite sure about that, Tommy. I *know*. You'd keep a child out of it."

"I withdraw," said Tommy. "I'll give you Mrs. Sprot and Miss Minton, but I'm not so sure about Mrs. Cayley."

"No, she might be a possibility. Because she really does overdo it. I mean there can't be many women *quite* as idiotic as she seems."

"I have often noticed that being a devoted wife saps the intellect," murmured Tommy.

"And where have you noticed that?" demanded Tuppence.

"Not from you, Tuppence. Your devotion has never reached those lengths."

"For a man," said Tuppence kindly, "you don't really make an undue fuss when you are ill."

Tommy reverted to a survey of possibilities.

"Cayley," said Tommy thoughtfully. "There might be something fishy about Cayley."

"Yes, there might. Then there's Mrs. O'Rourke."

"What do you feel about her?"

"I don't quite know. She's disturbing. Rather *fee fo fum*, if you know what I mean."

"Yes, I think I know. But I rather fancy that's just the predatory note. She's that kind of woman."

Tuppence said slowly:

"She—notices things."

She was remembering the remark about knitting.

"Then there's Bletchley," said Tommy.

"I've hardly spoken to him. He's definitely your chicken."

"I *think* he's just the ordinary pukka old school type. I *think* so."

"That's just it," said Tuppence, answering a stress rather than actual words. "The worst of this sort of show is that you look at quite ordinary everyday people and twist them to suit your morbid requirements."

"I've tried a few experiments on Bletchley," said Tommy.

"What sort of thing? I've got some experiments in mind myself."

"Well—just gentle ordinary little traps—about dates and places—all that sort of thing."

"Could you condescend from the general to the particular?"

"Well, say we're talking of duck shooting. He mentions the Fayum—good sport there such and such a year, such and such a month. Some other time I mention Egypt in quite a different connection. Mummies, Tutankhamen, something like that—has he seen that stuff? When was he there? Check up on the answers. Or P. & O. boats—I mention the names of one or two, say So-and-so was a comfortable boat. He mentions some trip or other, later I check that. Nothing important, or anything that puts him on his guard— just a check up on accuracy."

"And so far he hasn't slipped up in any way?"

"Not once. And that's a pretty good test, let me tell you, Tuppence."

"Yes, but I suppose *if* he was N, he *would* have his story quite pat."

"Oh, yes—the main outlines of it. But it's not so easy not to trip up on unimportant details. And then occasionally you remember too much—more, that is, than a bona fide person would do. An ordinary person doesn't usually remember offhand whether they took a certain shooting trip in 1926 or 1927. They have to think a bit and search their memory."

"But so far you haven't caught Bletchley out?"

"So far he's responded in a perfectly normal manner."

"Result—negative."

"Exactly."

"Now," said Tuppence. "I'll tell you some of my ideas." And she proceeded to do so.

THREE

On her way home, Mrs. Blenkensop stopped at the post office. She bought stamps and on her way out, went into one of the public call boxes. There she rang up a certain number, asked for "Mr. Faraday," and held a short conversation with him. She came out smiling and walked slowly homewards, stopping on the way to purchase some knitting wool.

It was a pleasant afternoon with a light breeze. Tuppence curbed the natural energy of her own brisk trot to that leisurely pace that accorded with her conception of the part of Mrs. Blenkensop. Mrs. Blenkensop had nothing on earth to do with herself except knit (not too well) and write letters to her boys. She was always writing letters to her boys—sometimes she left them about half finished.

Tuppence came slowly up the hill towards Sans Souci. Since it was not a through road (it ended at Smugglers' Rest, Commander Haydock's house) there was never much traffic—a few tradesmen's vans in the morning. Tuppence passed house after house, amusing herself by noting their names. Bella Vista (inaccurately named, since the merest glimpse of the sea was to be obtained, and the main view was the vast Victorian bulk of Edenholme on the other side of the road). Karachi was the next house. After that came

Shirley Tower. Then Sea View (appropriate this time), Castle Clare (somewhat grandiloquent, since it was a small house), Trelawny, a rival establishment to that of Mrs. Perenna, and finally the vast maroon bulk of Sans Souci.

It was just as she came near to it that Tuppence became aware of a woman standing by the gate peering inside. There was something tense and viligant about the figure.

Almost unconsciously, Tuppence softened the sound of her own footsteps, stepping cautiously upon her toes.

It was not until she was close behind her, that the woman heard her and turned. Turned with a start.

She was a tall woman, poorly, even meanly dressed, but her face was unusual. She was not young—probably between forty and fifty—but there was a contrast between her face and the way she was dressed. She was fair-haired, with wide cheekbones and had been—indeed still was—beautiful. Just for a minute Tuppence had a feeling that the woman's face was somehow familiar to her, but the feeling faded. It was not, she thought, a face easily forgotten.

The woman was obviously startled, and the flash of alarm that flitted across her face was not lost on Tuppence. (Something odd here?)

Tuppence said:

"Excuse me, are you looking for someone?"

The woman spoke in a slow foreign voice, pronouncing the words carefully as though she had learned them by heart.

"This 'ouse is Sans Souci?"

"Yes. I live here. Did you want someone?"

There was an infinitesimal pause, then the woman said:

"You can tell me, please. There is a Mr. Rosenstein there, no?"

"Mr. Rosenstein?" Tuppence shook her head. "No. I'm afraid not. Perhaps he has been there and left. Shall I ask for you?"

But the strange woman made a quick gesture of refusal. She said:

"No—no. I make mistake. Excuse, please."

Then, quickly, she turned and walked rapidly down the hill again.

Tuppence stood staring after her. For some reason, her suspicions were aroused. There was a contrast between the woman's manner and her words. Tuppence had an idea that "Mr. Rosenstein" was a fiction, that the woman had seized at the first name that came into her head.

Tuppence hesitated a minute, then she started down the hill after the other. What she could only describe as a "hunch" made her want to follow the woman.

Presently, however, she stopped. To follow would be to draw attention to herself in a rather marked manner. She had clearly been on the point of entering Sans Souci when she spoke to the woman; to reappear on her trail would be to arouse suspicion that Mrs. Blenkensop was something other than appeared on the surface—that is to say if this strange woman was indeed a member of the enemy plot.

No, at all costs Mrs. Blenkensop must remain what she seemed.

Tuppence turned and retraced her steps up the hill. She entered Sans Souci and paused in the hall. The house seemed deserted, as was usual early in the afternoon. Betty was having her nap, the elder members were either resting or had gone out.

Then, as Tuppence stood in the dim hall thinking over her recent encounter, a faint sound came to her ears. It was a sound she knew quite well—the faint echo of a ting.

The telephone at Sans Souci was in the hall. The sound that Tuppence had just heard was the sound made when the receiver of an extension is taken off or replaced. There was one extension in the house—in Mrs. Perenna's bedroom.

Tommy might have hesitated. Tuppence did not hesitate for a minute. Very gently and carefully she lifted off the receiver and put it to her ear.

Someone was using the extension. It was a man's voice. Tuppence heard:

"—everything going well. On the fourth, then, as arranged."

A woman's voice said:

"Yes, carry on."

There was a click as the receiver was replaced.

Tuppence stood there frowning. Was that Mrs. Perenna's voice? Difficult to say with only those three words to go upon. If there had been only a little more to the conversation. It might, of course, be quite an ordinary conversation —certainly there was nothing in the words she had overheard to indicate otherwise.

A shadow obscured the light from the door. Tuppence jumped and replaced the receiver as Mrs. Perenna spoke.

"Such a pleasant afternoon. Are you going out, Mrs. Blenkensop, or have you just come in?"

So it was not Mrs. Perenna who had been speaking from Mrs. Perenna's room. Tuppence murmured something about having had a pleasant walk and moved to the staircase.

Mrs. Perenna moved along the hall after her. She seemed bigger than usual. Tuppence was conscious of her as a strong athletic woman.

She said:

"I must get my things off," and hurried up the stairs. As she turned the corner of the landing she collided with Mrs. O'Rourke, whose vast bulk barred the top of the stairs.

"Dear, dear, now, Mrs. Blenkensop, it's a great hurry you seem to be in."

She did not move aside, just stood there smiling down at Tuppence just below her. There was, as always, a frightening quality about Mrs. O'Rourke's smile.

And suddenly, for no reason, Tuppence felt afraid.

The big smiling Irishwoman, with her deep voice, barring her way and below Mrs. Perenna closing in at the foot of the stairs.

Tuppence glanced over her shoulder. Was it her fancy that there was something definitely menacing in Mrs. Perenna's upturned face? Absurd, she told herself, absurd. In broad daylight—in a commonplace seaside boarding house. But the house was so very quiet. Not a sound. And she herself here on the stairs between the two of them. Surely there *was* something a little queer in Mrs. O'Rourke's smile—some fixed ferocious quality about it. Tuppence thought wildly, "Like a cat with a mouse."

And then suddenly the tension broke. A little figure darted along the top landing uttering shrill squeals of mirth. Little Betty Sprot in vest and knickers, darting past Mrs. O'Rourke, shouting happily "Peek Bo," as she flung herself on Tuppence.

The atmosphere had changed. Mrs. O'Rourke, a big genial figure, was crying out:

"Ah, the darlin'. It's a great girl she's getting."

Below, Mrs. Perenna had turned away to the door that led into the kitchen. Tuppence, Betty's hand clasped in hers, passed Mrs. O'Rourke and ran along the passage to where Mrs. Sprot was waiting to scold the truant.

Tuppence went in with the child.

She felt a queer sense of relief at the domestic atmosphere—the child's clothes lying about, the woolly toys, the painted crib, the sheeplike and somewhat unattractive face of Mr. Sprot in its frame on the dressing table, the burble of Mrs. Sprot's denunciation of laundry prices and really she thought Mrs. Perenna was a little unfair in refusing to sanction guests having their own electric irons—

All so normal, so reassuring, so everyday.

And yet—just now—on the stairs.

"Nerves," said Tuppence to herself. "Just nerves!"

But had it been nerves? Someone *had* been telephoning from Mrs. Perenna's room. Mrs. O'Rourke? Surely a very odd thing to do. It ensured, of course, that you would not be overheard by the household.

It must have been, Tuppence thought, a very short conversation. The merest brief exchange of words.

Everything going well. On the fourth as arranged.

It might mean nothing—or a good deal.

The fourth. Was that a date? The fourth, say, of a month?

Or it might mean the fourth seat, or the fourth lamp-post, or the fourth breakwater—impossible to know.

It might just conceivably mean the Forth Bridge. There had been an attempt to blow that up in the last War.

Did it mean anything at all?

It might quite easily have been the confirmation of some perfectly ordinary appointment. Mrs. Perenna might have told Mrs. O'Rourke she could use the telephone in her bedroom any time she wanted to do so.

And the atmosphere on the stairs, that tense moment, might have been just her own overwrought nerves . . .

The quiet house—the feeling that there was something sinister—something evil . . .

"Stick to facts, Mrs. Blenkensop," said Tuppence sternly. "And get on with your job."

5

Commander Haydock turned out to be a most genial host. He welcomed Mr. Meadowes and Major Bletchley with enthusiasm and insisted on showing the former "all over my little place."

Smugglers' Rest had been originally a couple of coast-guards' cottages standing on the cliff overlooking the sea. There was a small cove below, but the access to it was perilous, only to be attempted by adventurous boys.

Then the cottages had been bought by a London business man who had thrown them into one and attempted half-heartedly to make a garden. He had come down occasionally for short periods in summer.

After that the cottages had remained empty for some years, being let with a modicum of furniture to summer visitors.

"Then in 1926," explained Haydock, "it was sold to a man called Hahn. He was a German, and if you ask me, he was neither more nor less than a spy."

Tommy's ears quickened.

"That's interesting," he said, putting down the glass from which he had been sipping sherry.

"Damned thorough fellows they are," said Haydock. "Getting ready even then for this show—at least that is my opinion. Look at the situation of this place. Perfect for signalling out to sea. Cove below where you could land a motor-boat. Completely isolated, owing to the contour of the cliff. Oh, yes, don't tell me that fellow Hahn wasn't a German agent."

Major Bletchley said:

"Of course he was."

"What happened to him?" asked Tommy.

"Ah!" said Haydock, "thereby hangs a tale. Hahn spent a lot of money on this place. He had a way cut down to the beach for one thing—concrete steps—expensive business. Then he had the whole of the house done over—bathrooms, every expensive gadget you can imagine. And who did he set to do all this? Not local men. No, a firm from London, so it was said—but a lot of the men who came down were foreigners. Some of them *didn't speak a word of English*. Don't you agree with me that that sounds extremely fishy?"

"A little odd, certainly," agreed Tommy.

"I was in the neighbourhood myself at the time, living in a bungalow, and I got interested in what this fellow was up to. I used to hang about to watch the workmen. Now I'll tell you this—they didn't like it—they didn't like it at all. Once or twice they were quite threatening about it. Why should they be if everything was all square and aboveboard?"

Bletchley nodded agreement.

"You ought to have gone to the authorities," he said.

"Just what I did do, my dear fellow. Made a positive nuisance of myself pestering the police."

He poured himself out another drink.

"And what did I get for my pains? Polite inattention. Blind and deaf, that's what we were in this country. Another War with Germany was out of the question—there was peace in Europe—our relations with Germany were excellent. Natural sympathy between us nowadays. I was regarded as an old fossil, a War maniac, a diehard old sailor. What was the good of pointing out to people that the Germans were building the finest Air Force in Europe and not just to fly round and have picnics!"

Major Bletchley said explosively:

"Nobody believed it! Damned fools! Peace in our time. Appeasement. All a lot of blah!"

Haydock said, his face redder than usual with suppressed anger: "A War-monger, that's what they called me. The sort of chap, they said, who was an obstacle to peace. Peace! I knew what our Hun friends were at! And mind this, they

prepare things a long time beforehand. I was convinced that
Mr. Hahn was up to no good. I didn't like his foreign workmen. I didn't like the way he was spending money on this
place. I kept on badgering away at people."

"Stout fellow," said Bletchley appreciatively.

"And finally," said the Commander, "I began to make
an impression. We had a new Chief Constable down here—
retired soldier. And he had the sense to listen to me. His
fellows began to nose around. Sure enough, Hahn de-
camped. Just slipped out and disappeared one fine night.
The police went over this place with a search warrant. In a
safe which had been built-in in the dining room they found
a wireless transmitter and some pretty damaging documents.
Also a big store place under the garage for petrol—great
tanks. I can tell you I was cock-a-hoop over that. Fellows
at the club used to rag me about by German Spy complex.
They dried up after that. Trouble with us in this country is
that we're so absurdly unsuspicious."

"It's a crime. Fools—that's what we are—fools. Why
don't we intern all these refugees?" Major Bletchley was
well away.

"End of the story was I bought the place when it came
into the market," continued the Commander, not to be side-
tracked from his pet story. "Come in and have a look round,
Meadowes?"

"Thanks. I'd like to."

Commander Haydock was as full of zest as a boy as he
did the honours of the establishment. He threw open the
big safe in the dining room to show where the secret wireless had been found. Tommy was taken out to the garage and
was shown where the big petrol tanks had been concealed,
and finally, after a superficial glance at the two excellent
bathrooms, the special lighting, and the various kitchen
"gadgets," he was taken down the steep concreted path to
the little cove beneath, whilst Commander Haydock told
him all over again how extremely useful the whole layout
would be to an enemy in War time.

He was taken into the cave which gave the place its name
and Haydock pointed out enthusiastically how it could
have been used.

Major Bletchley did not accompany the two men on their tour, but remained peacefully sipping his drink on the terrace. Tommy gathered that the Commander's spy hunt with its successful issue was that good gentleman's principal topic of conversation and that his friends had heard it many times.

In fact, Major Bletchley said as much when they were walking down to Sans Souci a little later.

"Good fellow, Haydock," he said. "But he's not content to let a good thing alone. We've heard all about that business again and again until we're sick of it. He's as proud of the whole bag of tricks up there as a cat of its kittens."

The simile was not too far-fetched, and Tommy assented with a smile.

The conversation then turning to Major Bletchley's own successful unmasking of a dishonest bearer in 1923, Tommy's attention was free to pursue its own inward line of thought punctuated by sympathetic "Not reallys?"— "You don't say so?" and "What an extraordinary business!" which was all Major Bletchley needed in the way of encouragement.

More than ever now, Tommy felt that when the dying Farquhar had mentioned Sans Souci he had been on the right track. Here, in this out of the world spot, preparations had been made a long time beforehand. The arrival of the German Hahn and his extensive installation showed clearly enough that this particular part of the coast had been selected for a rallying point, a focus of enemy activity.

That particular game had been defeated by the unexpected activity of the suspicious Commander Haydock. Round One had gone to Britain. But supposing that Smugglers' Rest had been only the first outpost of a complicated scheme of attack? Smugglers' Rest, that is to say, had represented sea communications. Its beach, inaccessible save for the path down from above, would lend itself admirably to the plan. But it was only a part of the whole.

Defeated on that part of the plan by Haydock, what had been the enemy's response? Might not he have fallen back upon the next best thing—that is to say, Sans Souci? The exposure of Hahn had come about four years ago. Tommy had an idea, from what Sheila Perenna had said, that it was very soon after that that Mrs. Perenna had returned to England and bought Sans Souci. The next move in the game?

It would seem, therefore, that Leahampton was definitely an enemy center—that there were already installations and affiliations in the neighborhood.

His spirits rose. The depression engendered by the harmless and futile atmosphere of Sans Souci disappeared. Innocent as it seemed, that innocence was no more than skin deep. Behind that innocuous mask things were going on.

And the focus of it all, so far as Tommy could judge, was Mrs. Perenna. The first thing to do was to know more about Mrs. Perenna, to penetrate behind her apparently simple routine of running her boarding establishment. Her correspondence, her acquaintances, her social or War working activities—somewhere in all these must lie the essence of her real activities. If Mrs. Perenna was the renowned woman agent, M, then it was she who controlled the whole of the Fifth Column activities in this country. Her identity would be known to few—only to those at the top. But communications she must have with her chiefs of staff and it was those communications that he and Tuppence had got to tap.

At the right moment, as Tommy saw well enough, Smugglers' Rest could be seized and held—by a few stalwarts operating from Sans Souci. That moment was not yet, but it might be very near.

Once the German Army was established in control of the channel ports in France and Belgium, they could concentrate on the invasion and subjugation of Britain, and things were certainly going very badly in France at the moment.

Britain's Navy was all-powerful on the sea, so the attack must come by air and by internal treachery—and if the threads of internal treachery were in Mrs. Perenna's keeping, there was no time to lose.

Major Bletchley's words chimed in with his thoughts:

"I saw, you know, that there was no time to lose. I got hold of Abdul, my sayce—good fellow, Abdul—"

The story droned on.

Tommy was thinking:

"Why Leahampton? Any reason? It's out of the main

stream—bit of a backwater. Conservative, old-fashioned. All those points make it desirable. Is there anything else?"

There was a stretch of flat agricultural country behind it, running inland. A lot of pasture. Suitable, therefore, for the landing of troop-carrying airplanes or of parachute troops. But that was true of many other places. There was also a big chemical works where, it might be noted, Carl von Deinim was employed.

Carl von Deinim. How did he fit in? Only too well. He was not, as Grant had pointed out, the real head. A cog, only, in the machine. Liable to suspicion and internment at any moment. But in the meantime, he might have accomplished what had been his task. He had mentioned to Tuppence that he was working on decontamination problems and on the immunizing of certain gases. There were probabilities there—probabilities unpleasant to contemplate.

Carl, Tommy decided (a little reluctantly) was in it. A pity, because he rather liked the fellow. Well, he was working for his country—taking his life in his hands. Tommy had respect for such an adversary—down him by all means —a firing party was the end, but you knew that when you took on your job.

It was the people who betrayed their own land—from within—that really aroused a slow vindictive passion in him. By God, he'd get them!

—"And that's how I got them!" The Major wound up his story triumphantly. "Pretty smart bit of work, eh?"

Unblushingly Tommy said:

"Most ingenious thing I've heard in my life, Major."

TWO

Mrs. Blenkensop was reading a letter on thin foreign paper, stamped outside with the censor's mark.

"Dear Raymond," she murmured. "I was so happy about him out in Egypt, and now, it seems, there is a big change round. All *very* secret, of course, and he can't *say* anything —just that there really is a marvellous plan and that I'm to be ready for some *big surprises* soon. I'm glad to know where he's being sent, but I really don't see why——"

Bletchley grunted.

"Surely he's not allowed to tell you that?"

Tuppence gave a deprecating laugh and looked round the breakfast table as she folded up her precious letter.

"Oh! We have our methods," she said archly. "Dear Raymond knows that if only I know where he is or where he's going I don't worry quite so much. It's quite a simple way, too. Just a certain word, you know, and after it the initial letters of the next words spell out the place. Of course it makes rather a funny sentence sometimes—but Raymond is really most ingenious. I'm sure *nobody* would notice."

Little murmurs arose round the table. The moment was well chosen, everybody happened to be at the breakfast table together for once.

Bletchley, his face rather red, said:

"You'll excuse me, Mrs. Blenkensop, but that's a damned foolish thing to do. Movements of troops and air squadrons are just what the Germans want to know."

"Oh, but I never tell anyone," cried Tuppence. "I'm very, very careful."

"All the same it's an unwise thing to do—and your boy will get into trouble over it some day."

"Oh, I do hope not. I'm his *mother,* you see. A mother *ought* to know."

"Indeed and I think you're right," boomed out Mrs. O'Rourke. "Wild horses wouldn't drag the information from you—we know that."

"Letters can be read," said Bletchley.

"I'm very careful never to leave letters lying about," said Tuppence with an air of outraged dignity. "I always keep them locked up."

Bletchley shook his head doubtfully.

THREE

It was a grey morning with the wind blowing coldly from the sea. Tuppence was alone at the far end of the beach.

She took from her bag two letters that she had just called for at a small news agent's in the town.

She opened them.

DEAREST MOTHER,

Lots of funny things I could tell you only I mustn't. We're putting up a good show, I think. Five German planes before breakfast is today's market quotation. Bit of a mess at the moment and all that, but we'll get there all right in the end.

It's the way they machine gun the poor civilian devils on the roads that gets me. It makes us all see red. Gus and Trundles want to be remembered to you. They're still going strong.

Don't worry about me. I'm all right. Wouldn't have missed this show for the world. Love to old Carrot Top—have the W.C. given him a job yet?

Yours ever—

DEREK

Tuppence's eyes were very bright and shining as she read and re-read this.

Then she opened the other letter.

DEAREST MUM,

How's old Aunt Gracie? Going strong? I think you're wonderful to stick it. I couldn't.

No news. My job's very interesting, but so hush-hush I can't tell you about it. But I really do feel I'm doing something worth while. Don't fret about not getting any War work to do—it's so silly all these elderly women rushing about wanting to *do* things. They only really want people who are young and efficient. I wonder how Carrots is getting on at his job up in Scotland? Just filling up forms, I suppose. Still he'll be happy to feel he is doing something.

Lots of love.

DEBORAH

Tuppence smiled.

She folded the letters, smoothed them lovingly and then under the shelter of a breakwater she struck a match and set them on fire. She waited until they were reduced to ashes.

Taking out her fountain pen and a small writing pad she wrote rapidly.

LANGHERNE,

CORNWALL.

DEAREST DEB,

It seems so remote from the War here that I can hardly believe there is a War going on. Very glad to get your letter and know that your work is interesting.

Aunt Gracie has grown much more feeble and very hazy in her mind. I think she is glad to have me here. She talks a good deal about the old days and sometimes, I think, confuses me with my own mother. They are growing more vegetables than usual—have turned the rose garden into potatoes. I help old Sikes a bit. It makes me feel I am doing something in the War. Your father seems a bit disgruntled but I think, as you say, he too is glad to be doing something.

Love from your

TUPPENNY MOTHER

She took a fresh sheet.

DARLING DEREK,

A great comfort to get your letter. Send field post-cards often if you haven't time to write.

I've come down to be with Aunt Gracie a bit. She is very feeble. She will talk of you as though you were seven and gave me ten shillings yesterday to send you as a tip.

I'm still on the shelf and nobody wants my invaluable services! Extraordinary! Your father, as I told you, has got a job in the Ministry of Requirements. He is up North somewhere. Better than nothing, but not what he wanted, poor old Carrot Top. Still I suppose we've got to be humble and take a back seat and leave the War to you young idiots.

I won't say "Take care of yourself," because I

gather that the whole point is that you should do just the opposite. But don't go and be stupid.

Lots of love.

TUPPENCE

She put the letters into envelopes, addressed and stamped them and posted them on her way back to Sans Souci.

As she reached the bottom of the cliff her attention was caught by two figures standing talking a little way up.

Tuppence stopped dead. It was the same woman she had seen yesterday and talking to her was Carl von Deinim.

Regretfully Tuppence noted the fact that there was no cover. She could not get near them unseen and overhear what was being said.

Moreover, at that moment the young German turned his head and saw her. Rather abruptly, the two figures parted. The woman came rapidly down the hill, crossing the road and passing Tuppence on the other side.

Carl von Deinim waited until Tuppence came up to him. Then, gravely and politely, he wished her good morning.

Tuppence said immediately:

"What a very odd looking woman that was to whom you were talking, Mr. von Deinim."

"Yes. It is a Central European type. She is a Czech."

"Really? A—a friend of yours?"

Tuppence's tone was a very good copy of the inquisitive voice of Aunt Gracie in her younger days.

"Not at all," said Carl stiffly. "I never saw the woman before."

"Oh, really. I thought—" Tuppence paused artistically.

"She asks me only for a direction. I speak German to her because she does not understand much English."

"I see. And she was asking the way somewhere?"

"She asked me if I knew a Mrs. Gottlieb near here. I do not, and she says she has, perhaps, got the name of the house wrong."

"I see," said Tuppence thoughtfully.

Mr. Rosenstein. Mrs. Gottlieb.

She stole a swift glance at Carl von Deinim. He was walking beside her with a set stiff face.

Tuppence felt a definite suspicion of this strange woman.
And she felt almost convinced that when she had first caught
sight of them, the woman and Carl had been already talking
some time together.

Carl von Deinim?

Carl and Sheila that morning. *"You must be careful. . . ."*

Tuppence thought:

"I hope—I hope these young things *aren't* in it!"

Soft, she told herself, middle-aged and soft! That's what
she was! The Nazi creed was a youth creed. Nazi agents
would in all probability be young. Carl and Sheila. Tommy
said Sheila wasn't in it. Yes, but Tommy was a man, and
Sheila was beautiful with a queer breath-taking beauty.

Carl and Sheila, and behind them that enigmatic figure:
Mrs. Perenna. Mrs. Perenna, sometimes the voluble, commonplace, guest house hostess, sometimes, for fleeting
minutes, a tragic violent personality.

Tuppence went slowly upstairs to her bedroom.

That evening, when Tuppence went to bed, she pulled
out the long drawer of her bureau. At one side of it was a
small japanned box with a flimsy cheap lock. Tuppence
slipped on gloves, unlocked the box, and opened it. A pile of
letters lay inside. On the top was the one received that morning from "Raymond." Tuppence unfolded it with due pre-
cautions.

Then her lips set grimly. There had been an eyelash in
the fold of the paper this morning. The eyelash was not there
now.

She went to the washstand. There was a little bottle
labelled innocently: "Grey powder" with a dose.

Adroitly Tuppence dusted a little of the powder onto the
letter and onto the surface of the glossy japanned enamel
of the box.

There were no fingerprints on either of them.

Again Tuppence nodded her head with a certain grim
satisfaction.

For there should have been fingerprints—her own.

A servant might have read letters out of curiosity, though

it seemed unlikely—certainly unlikely that she should have gone to the trouble of finding a key to fit the box.

But a servant would not think of wiping off fingerprints.

Mrs. Perenna? Sheila? Somebody else? Somebody, at least, who was interested in the movements of British armed forces.

FOUR

Tuppence's plan of campaign had been simple in its outlines. First, a general sizing up of probabilities and possibilities. Second, an experiment to determine whether there was or was not an inmate of Sans Souci who was interested in troop movements and anxious to conceal the fact.

Third—who that person was?

It was concerning that third operation that Tuppence pondered as she lay in bed the following morning. Her train of thought was slightly hampered by Betty Sprot, who had pranced in at an early hour, preceding indeed the cup of somewhat tepid inky liquid known as Morning Tea.

Betty was both active and voluble. She had taken a great attachment to Tuppence. She climbed up on the bed and thrust an extremely tattered picture book under Tuppence's nose, commanding with brevity:

"Wead."

Tuppence read obediently:

"Goosey, goosey gander, whither will you wander?
Upstairs, downstairs, in my lady's chamber."

Betty rolled with mirth—repeating in an ecstasy:

"Uptares—uptares—uptares—" and then with a sudden climax: *"Down—"* and proceeded to roll off the bed with a thump.

This proceeding was repeated several times until it palled. Then Betty crawled about the floor, playing with Tuppence's shoes and muttering busily to herself in her own particular idiom:

"Ag da—bah pit—soo—soo dah—putch—"

Released to fly back to its own perplexities, Tuppence's
mind forgot the child. The words of the nursery rhyme
seemed to mock her.

Goosey, goosey gander, whither shall ye wander?

Whither indeed? Goosey, that was her, Gander was
Tommy. It was, at any rate, what they appeared to be! Tuppence had the heartiest contempt for Mrs. Blenkensop. Mr.
Meadowes, she thought, was a little better—stolid, British,
unimaginative—quite incredibly stupid. Both of them, she
hoped, fitting nicely into the background of Sans Souci. Both
such possible people to be there.

All the same, one must not relax—a slip was so easy. She
had made one the other day—nothing that mattered, but
just a sufficient indication to warn her to be careful. Such an
easy approach to intimacy and good relations—an indiffer-
ent knitter asking for guidance. But she had forgotten that
one evening, her fingers had slipped into their own practised
efficiency, the needles clicking busily with the even note of
the experienced knitter. And Mrs. O'Rourke had noticed it.
Since then, she had carefully struck a medium course—not
so clumsy as she had been at first—but not so rapid as she
could be.

"Ag boo bate?" demanded Betty. She reiterated the question: "Ag boo bate?"

"Lovely, darling," said Tuppence absently. "Beautiful."

Satisfied Betty relapsed into murmurs again.

Her next step, Tuppence thought, could be managed easily
enough. That is to say with the connivance of Tommy. She
saw exactly how to do it—

Lying there planning, time slipped by. Mrs. Sprot came
in, breathless, to seek for Betty.

"Oh, here she is. I couldn't think where she had got to.
Oh, Betty, you naughty girl—Oh, dear, Mrs. Blenkensop, I
am so sorry."

Tuppence sat up in bed. Betty, with an angelic face, was
contemplating her handiwork.

She had removed all the laces from Tuppence's shoes and

had immersed them in a glass of water. She was prodding them now with a gleeful finger.

Tuppence laughed and cut short Mrs. Sprot's apologies.

"How frightfully funny. Don't worry, Mrs. Sprot, they'll recover all right. It's my fault. I should have noticed what she was doing. She was rather quiet."

"I know." Mrs. Sprot sighed. "Whenever they're quiet, it's a bad sign. I'll get you some more laces this morning, Mrs. Blenkensop."

"Don't bother," said Tuppence. "They'll dry none the worse."

Mrs. Sprot bore Betty away and Tuppence got up to put her plan into execution.

6

Tommy looked rather gingerly at the packet that Tuppence thrust upon him.

"Is this it?"

"Yes. Be careful. Don't get it over you."

Tommy took a delicate sniff at the packet and replied with energy:

"No, indeed. What is this frightful stuff?"

"Asafoetida," replied Tuppence. "A pinch of that and you will wonder why your boy friend is no longer attentive, as the advertisements say."

"Shades of B.O.," murmured Tommy.

Shortly after that, various incidents occurred.

The first was the Smell in Mr. Meadowes' room.

Mr. Meadowes, not a complaining man by nature, spoke about it mildly at first, then with increasing firmness.

Mrs. Perenna was summoned into conclave. With all the will in the world to resist, she had to admit that there was a smell. A pronounced, unpleasant smell. Perhaps, she suggested, the gas tap of the fire was leaking.

Bending down and sniffing dubiously, Tommy remarked that he did not think the smell came from there. Nor from under the floor. He himself thought, definitely—a dead rat.

Mrs. Perenna admitted that she had heard of such things —but she was sure there were no rats at Sans Souci. Perhaps a mouse—though she herself had never seen a mouse there.

Mr. Meadowes said with firmness that he thought the smell indicated at least a rat—and he added, still more firmly, that he was not going to sleep another night in the room until the matter had been seen to. He would ask Mrs. Perenna to change his room.

Mrs. Perenna said, Of course, she had just been about to suggest the same thing. She was afraid that the only room vacant was rather a small one and unfortunately it had no sea view, but if Mr. Meadowes did not mind that—

Mr. Meadowes did not. His only wish was to get away from the smell. Mrs. Perenna thereupon accompanied him to a small bedroom, the door of which happened to be just opposite the door of Mrs. Blenkensop's room, and summoned the adenoidal, semi-idiotic Beatrice to "move Mr. Meadowes' things." She would, she explained, send for "a man" to take up the floor and search for the origin of the smell.

Matters were settled satisfactorily on this basis.

TWO

The second incident was Mr. Meadowes' hay fever. That was what he called it at first. Later he admitted doubtfully that he might just possibly have caught cold. He sneezed a good deal, and his eyes ran. If there was a faint elusive suggestion of raw onion floating in the breeze in the vicinity of Mr. Meadowes' large silk handkerchief nobody noticed the fact and indeed a pungent amount of eau de cologne masked the more penetrating odour.

Finally, defeated by incessant sneezing and nose-blowing, Mr. Meadowes retired to bed for the day.

It was on the morning of that day that Mrs. Blenkensop received a letter from her son, Douglas. So excited and thrilled was Mrs. Blenkensop that everybody at Sans Souci heard about it. The letter had not been censored at all, she explained, because fortunately one of Douglas's friends coming home on leave had brought it, so for once Douglas had been able to write quite fully.

"And it just shows," declared Mrs. Blenkensop, wagging her head sagely, "how little we really know of what is going on."

After breakfast she went upstairs to her room, opened the japanned box and put the letter away. Between the folded pages were some unnoticeable grains of rice powder. She closed the box again, pressing her fingers firmly on its surface.

As she left her room she coughed, and from opposite came the sound of a highly histrionic sneeze.

Tuppence smiled and proceeded downstairs.

She had already made known her intention of going up to London for the day—to see her lawyer on some business and to do a little shopping.

Now she was given a good send-off by the assembled boarders and entrusted with various commissions—"only if you have time, of course."

Major Bletchley held himself aloof from this female chatter. He was reading his paper and uttering appropriate comments aloud. "Damned swines of Germans. Machine gunning civilian refugees on the roads. Damned brutes. If I were our people—"

Tuppence left him still outlining what he would do if he were in charge of operations.

She made a detour through the garden to ask Betty Sprot what she would like as a present from London.

Betty, ecstatically clasping a snail in two hot hands, gurgled appreciatively. In response to Tuppence's suggestions "A pussy? A picture book? Some coloured chalks to draw with?" Betty decided, "Betty dwar." So the coloured chalks were noted down on Tuppence's list.

As she passed on, meaning to rejoin the drive by the path at the end of the garden, she came unexpectedly upon Carl von Deinim. He was standing leaning on the wall. His hands were clenched, and as Tuppence approached he turned on her, his usually impassive face convulsed with emotion.

Tuppence paused involuntarily and asked:

"Is anything the matter?"

"Ach, yes, everything is the matter." His voice was hoarse and unnatural. "You have a saying here that a thing is neither fish, flesh, fowl nor good red herring, have you not?"

Tuppence nodded.

Carl went on bitterly:

"That is what I am. It cannot go on, that is what I say. It

cannot go on. It would be best, I think, to end everything."

"What do you mean?"

The young man said:

"You have spoken kindly to me. You would, I think, understand. I fled from my own country because of injustice and cruelty. I came here to find freedom. I hated Nazi Germany. But alas, I am still a German. Nothing can alter that."

Tuppence murmured:

"You must have difficulties, I know—"

"It is not that. I am a German, I tell you. In my heart— in my feeling. Germany is still my country. When I read of German cities bombed, of German soldiers dying, of German aeroplanes brought down—they are my people who die. When that old fire-eating Major reads out from his paper, when he says 'those swine'—I am moved to fury—I cannot bear it."

He added quietly:

"And so I think it would be best, perhaps, to end it all. Yes, to end it."

Tuppence took hold of him firmly by the arm.

"Nonsense," she said robustly. "Of course you feel as you do. Anyone would. But you've got to stick it."

"I wish they would intern me. It would be easier so."

"Yes, probably it would. But in the meantime you're doing useful work—or so I've heard. Useful not only to England but to humanity. You're working on decontamination problems, aren't you?"

His face lit up slightly.

"Ah, yes, and I begin to have much success. A process very simple, easily made and not complicated to apply."

"Well," said Tuppence, "that's worth doing. Anything that mitigates suffering is worth while—and anything that's constructive and not destructive. Naturally we've got to call the other side names. They're doing just the same in Germany. Hundreds of Major Bletchleys—foaming at the mouth. I hate the Germans myself. 'The Germans,' I say, and feel waves of loathing. But when I think of individual Germans, mothers sitting anxiously waiting for news of their sons, and boys leaving home to fight, and peasants getting in the harvests, and little shopkeepers and some of the nice kindly German people I know, I feel quite different. I know then they are just human beings and that we're all feeling alike. That's the real thing. The other is just the War mask that you put on. It's a part of War—probably a necessary part—but it's ephemeral."

As she spoke she thought, as Tommy had done not long before, of Nurse Cavell's words: "Patriotism is not enough. I must have no hatred in my heart."

That saying of a most truly patriotic woman had always seemed to them both the high water mark of sacrifice.

Carl von Deinim took her hand and kissed it. He said:

"I thank you. What you say is good and true. I will have more fortitude."

"Oh, dear," thought Tuppence as she walked down the road into the town. "How very fortunate that the person I like best in this place should be a German. It makes everything cock-eyed!"

THREE

Tuppence was nothing if not thorough. Although she had no wish to go to London, she judged it wise to do exactly as she had said she was going to do. If she merely made an excursion somewhere for the day, somebody might see her and the fact would get round to Sans Souci.

No, Mrs. Blenkensop had said she was going to London and to London she must go.

She purchased a third return and was just leaving the booking office window when she ran into Sheila Perenna.

"Hullo," said Sheila. "Where are you off to? I just came to see about a parcel which seems to have gone astray."

Tuppence explained her plans.

"Oh, yes, of course," said Sheila carelessly. "I do remember you saying something about it, but I hadn't realized it was today you were going. I'll come and see you into the train."

Sheila was more animated than usual. She looked neither bad tempered nor sulky. She chatted quite amiably about small details of daily life at Sans Souci. She remained talking to Tuppence until the train left the station.

After waving from the window and watching the girl's figure recede, Tuppence sat down in her corner seat again and gave herself up to serious meditation.

Was it, she wondered, an accident that Sheila had happened to be at the station just at that time? Or was it a proof of enemy thoroughness? Did Mrs. Perenna want to make quite sure that the garrulous Mrs. Blenkensop really *had* gone to London?

It looked very much like it.

FOUR

It was not until the next day that Tuppence was able to have a conference with Tommy. They had agreed never to attempt to communicate with each other under the roof of Sans Souci.

Mrs. Blenkensop met Mr. Meadowes as the latter, his hay fever somewhat abated, was taking a gentle stroll on the front. They sat down on one of the promenade seats.

"Well?" said Tuppence.

Slowly, Tommy nodded his head. He looked rather unhappy.

"Yes," he said. "I got something. But, Lord, what a day. Perpetually with an eye to the crack of the door. I've got quite a stiff neck."

"Never mind your neck," said Tuppence unfeelingly. "Tell me."

"Well, the maids went in to do the bed and the room, of course. And Mrs. Perenna went in—but that was when the maids were there and she was just blowing them up about something. And the kid ran in once and came out with a woolly dog."

"Yes, yes. Anyone else?"

"One person," said Tommy slowly.

"Who?"

"Carl von Deinim."

"Oh." Tuppence felt a swift pang. So, after all—

"When?" she asked.

"Lunch time. He came out from the dining room early, came up to his room, then sneaked across the passage and into yours. He was there about a quarter of an hour."

He paused.

"That settles it, I think?"

Tuppence nodded.

Yes, it settled it all right. Carl von Deinim could have no reason for going into Mrs. Blenkensop's bedroom and remaining there for a quarter of an hour save one. His complicity was proved. He must be, Tuppence thought, a marvellous actor . . .

His words to her that morning had rung so very true. Well, perhaps they had been true in a way. To know when to use the truth was the essence of successful deception. Carl von Deinim was a patriot all right, he was an enemy agent working for his country. One could respect him for that. Yes—but destroy him too.

"I'm sorry," she said slowly.

"So am I," said Tommy. "He's a good chap."

Tuppence said:

"You and I might be doing the same thing in Germany."

Tommy nodded. Tuppence went on.

"Well, we know more or less where we are. Carl von Deinim working in with Sheila and her mother. Probably Mrs. Perenna is the big noise. Then there is that foreign woman who was talking to Carl yesterday. She's in it somehow."

"What do we do now?"

"We must go through Mrs. Perenna's room some time. There might be something there that would give us a hint. And we must tail her—see where she goes and whom she meets. Tommy, let's get Albert down here."

Tommy considered the point.

Some years ago, Albert, a page boy in a hotel, had joined forces with the young Beresfords and shared their adventures. Afterwards he had entered their service and been the sole domestic prop of the establishment. Some six years ago he had married and was now the proud proprietor of The Duck and Dog pub in South London.

Tuppence continued rapidly:

"Albert will be thrilled. We'll get him down here. He can stay at that pub near the station and he can shadow the Perennas for us—or anyone else."

"What about Mrs. Albert?"

"She was going to her mother in Wales with the children last Monday. Because of Air Raids. It all fits in perfectly."

"Yes, that's a good idea, Tuppence. Either of us following the woman about would be rather conspicuous. Albert will be perfect. Now another thing—I think we ought to watch out for that so-called Czech woman who was talking to Carl and hanging about here. It seems to me that she probably represents the other end of the business—and that's what we're anxious to find."

"Oh, yes, I do agree. She comes here for orders, or to take messages. Next time we see her, one of us must follow her and find out more about her."

"What about looking through Mrs. Perenna's room—and Carl's, too, I suppose?"

"I don't suppose you'll find anything in his. After all, as a German, the police are liable to search it and so he'd be careful not to have anything suspicious. The Perenna is going to be difficult. When she's out of the house, Sheila is often here, and there's Betty and Mrs. Sprot running about all over the landings, and Mrs. O'Rourke spends a lot of time in her bedroom."

She paused.

"Lunch time is the best."

"Master Carl's time?"

"Exactly. I could have a headache and go to my room— No, someone might come up and want to minister to me. I know, I'll just come in quietly before lunch and go up to my room without telling anyone. Then, after lunch, I can say I had a headache."

"Hadn't I better do it? My hay fever could recrudesce tomorrow."

"I think it had better be me. If I'm caught I could always say I was looking for aspirin or something. One of the gentlemen boarders in Mrs. Perenna's room would cause far more speculation."

Tommy grinned.

"Of a scandalous character."

Then the smile died. He looked grave and anxious.

"As soon as we can, old thing. The news is bad today. We must get on to something soon."

FIVE

Tommy continued his walk and presently entered the post office, where he put through a call to Mr. Grant, and reported "the recent operation was successful and our friend C is definitely involved."

Then he wrote a letter and posted it. It was addressed to Mr. Albert Batt, The Duck and Dog, Glamorgan St., Kensington.

Then he bought himself a weekly paper which professed to inform the English world of what was really going to happen and strolled innocently back in the direction of Sans Souci.

Presently he was hailed by the hearty voice of Commander Haydock leaning from his two seater car and shouting, "Hullo, Meadowes, want a lift?"

Tommy accepted the lift gratefully and got in.

"So you read that rag, do you?" demanded Haydock, glancing at the scarlet cover of the *Inside Weekly News*.

Mr. Meadowes displayed the slight confusion of all readers of the periodical in question when challenged.

"Awful rag," he agreed. "But sometimes, you know, they really do seem to know what's going on behind the scenes."

"And sometimes they're wrong."

"Oh, quite so."

"Truth of it is," said Commander Haydock, steering rather erratically round a one-way island and narrowly missing collision with a large van, "when the beggars are right, you remember it, and when they're wrong you forget it."

"Do you think there's any truth in this rumour about Stalin having approached us?"

"Wishful thinking, my boy, wishful thinking," said Commander Haydock. "The Russkys are as crooked as Hell and always have been. Don't trust 'em, that's what I say. Hear you've been under the weather?"

"Just a touch of hay fever. I get it about this time of year."

"Yes, of course. Never suffered from it myself, but I had a pal who did. Used to lay him out regularly every June. Feeling fit enough for a game of golf?"

Tommy said he'd like it very much.

"Right. What about tomorrow? Tell you what, I've got to go to a meeting about this Parashot business, raising a corps of local volunteers—jolly good idea, if you ask me. Time we were all made to pull our weight. So shall we have a round about six?"

"Thanks very much. I'd like to."

"Good. Then that's settled."

The Commander drew up abruptly at the gate of Sans Souci.

"How's the fair Sheila?" he asked.

"Quite well, I think. I haven't seen much of her."

Haydock gave his loud barking laugh.

"Not as much as you'd like to, I bet! Good looking girl, that, but damned rude. She sees too much of that German fellow. Damned unpatriotic, I call it. Daresay she's got no use for old fogies like you or me, but there are plenty of nice lads going about in our own services. Why take up with a bloody German? That sort of thing riles me."

Mr. Meadowes said:

"Be careful, he's just coming up the hill behind us."

"Don't care if he does hear! Rather hope he does. I'd like to kick Master Carl's behind for him. Any decent German's fighting for his country—not slinking over here to get out of it!"

"Well," said Tommy. "It's one less German to invade England at all events."

"You mean he's here already? Ha, ha! rather good, Meadowes! Not that I believe this tommyrot about invasion. We never have been invaded and never will be. We've got a Navy, thank God!"

With which patriotic announcement the Commander let in his clutch with a jerk and the car leaped forward up the hill to Smugglers' Rest.

SIX

Tuppence arrived at the gate of Sans Souci at twenty minutes to two. She turned off from the drive and went through the garden and into the house through the open drawing room window. A smell of Irish stew and the clatter of plates and murmur of voices came from afar. Sans Souci was hard at work on its midday meal.

Tuppence waited by the drawing room door until Martha, the maid, had passed across the hall and into the dining room, then she ran quickly up the stairs, shoeless.

She went into the room, put on her soft felt bedroom slippers, and then went along the landing and into Mrs. Perenna's room.

Once inside she looked round her and felt a certain distaste sweep over her. Not a nice job, this. Quite unpardonable if Mrs. Perenna was simply Mrs. Perenna. Prying into people's private affairs—

Tuppence shook herself, an impatient terrier shake that was a reminiscence of her girlhood. *There was a War on!*

She went over to the dressing table.

Quick and deft in her movements, she had soon gone through the contents of the drawers there. In the tall bureau, one of the drawers was locked. That seemed more promising.

Tommy had been entrusted with certain tools and had received some brief instruction on the manipulation of them. These indications he had passed on to Tuppence.

A deft twist or two of the wrist and the drawer yielded.

There was a cash box containing twenty pounds in notes and some piles of silver—also a jewel case. And there was a heap of papers. These last were what interested Tuppence most. Rapidly she went through them; necessarily it was a cursory glance. She could not afford time for more.

Papers relating to a mortgage on Sans Souci, a bank account, letters. Time flew past, Tuppence skimmed through the documents, concentrating furiously on anything that might bear a double meaning. Two letters from a friend in Italy, rambling discursive letters, seemingly quite harmless.

But possibly not so harmless as they sounded. A letter from one Simon Mortimer, of London—a dry business-like letter containing so little of moment that Tuppence wondered why it had been kept. Was Mr. Mortimer not so harmless as he seemed? At the bottom of the pile a letter in faded ink signed Pat and beginning *"This will be the last letter I'll be writing you, Eileen my darling—"*

No, not that! Tuppence could not bring herself to read that! She refolded it, tidied the letters on top of it and then, suddenly alert, pushed the drawer to—no time to re-lock it —and when the door opened and Mrs. Perenna came in, she was searching vaguely amongst the bottles on the washstand.

Mrs. Blenkensop turned a flustered, but foolish face towards her hostess.

"Oh, Mrs. Perenna, do forgive me. I came in with such a blinding headache, and I thought I would lie down on my bed with a little aspirin, and I couldn't find mine, so I thought you wouldn't mind—I know you must have some because you offered it to Miss Minton the other day."

Mrs. Perenna swept into the room. There was a sharpness in her voice as she said:

"Why, of course, Mrs. Blenkensop, why ever didn't you come and ask me?"

"Well, of course, yes, I should have done really. But I knew you were all at lunch, and I do so hate, you know, making a *fuss—*"

Passing Tuppence, Mrs. Perenna caught up the bottle of aspirin from the washstand.

"How many would you like?" she demanded crisply.

Mrs. Blenkensop accepted three. Escorted by Mrs. Perenna she crossed to her own room and hastily demurred to the suggestion of a hot water bottle.

Mrs. Perenna used her parting shot as she left the room.

"But you have some aspirin of your own, Mrs. Blenkensop. I've seen it."

Tuppence cried quickly:

"Oh, I know. I know I've got some somewhere, but, so stupid of me, I simply couldn't lay my hands on it."

Mrs. Perenna said, with a flash of her big white teeth:

"Well, have a good rest until tea time."

She went out, closing the door behind her. Tuppence
drew a deep breath, lying on her bed rigidly lest Mrs. Perenna should return.

Had the other suspected anything? Those teeth, so big
and white—the better to eat you with, my dear. Tuppence
always thought of that when she noticed those teeth. Mrs.
Perenna's hands, too, big, cruel-looking hands.

She had appeared to accept Tuppence's presence in her
bedroom quite naturally. But later she would find the bureau
drawer unlocked. Would she suspect then? Or would she
think she had left it unlocked herself by accident? One did
do such things. Had Tuppence been able to replace the
papers in such a way that they looked much the same as
before?

Surely, even if Mrs. Perenna did notice anything amiss
she would be more likely to suspect one of the servants
than she would "Mrs. Blenkensop." And if she did suspect
the latter, wouldn't it be a mere case of suspecting her of
undue curiosity? There were people, Tuppence knew, who
did poke and pry.

But then, if Mrs. Perenna were the renowned German
agent, M, she would be suspicious of counter espionage.

Had anything in her bearing revealed undue alertness?

She had seemed natural enough—only that one sharply
pointed remark about the aspirin.

Suddenly, Tuppence sat up on her bed. She remembered
that her aspirin, together with some iodine and a bottle of
soda mints were all together at the back of the writing table
drawer where she had shoved them when unpacking.

It would seem, therefore, that she was not the only person
to snoop in other people's rooms. Mrs. Perenna had got
there first.

7

On the following day Mrs. Sprot went up to London.

A few tentative remarks on her part had led immediately to various offers on the part of the inhabitants of Sans Souci to look after Betty.

When Mrs. Sprot, with many final adjurations to Betty to be a very good girl, had departed, Betty attached herself to Tuppence, who had elected to take morning duty.

"Play," said Betty. "Play hide seek."

She was talking more easily every day and had adopted a most fetching habit of laying her head on one side, fixing her interlocutor with a bewitching smile and murmuring:

"*Peese.*"

Tuppence had intended taking her for a walk, but it was raining hard, so the two of them adjourned to the bedroom where Betty led the way to the bottom drawer of the bureau where her playthings were kept.

"Hide Bonzo, shall we?" asked Tuppence.

But Betty had changed her mind and demanded instead:

"Wead me story."

Tuppence pulled out a rather tattered book from one end of the cupboard—to be interrupted by a squeal from Betty.

"No, no. Narsty . . . Bad . . ."

Tuppence stared at her in surprise and then down at the book, which was a coloured version of *Little Jack Horner*.

"Was Jack a bad boy?" she asked. "Because he pulled out a plum?"

Betty reiterated with emphasis:

"Ba-a-ad!" and with a terrific effort, "Dirrty!"

She seized the book from Tuppence and replaced it in
the line, then tugged out an identical book from the other
end of the shelf, announcing with a beaming face:

"K-k-klean ni-i-i-ice Jackorner!"

Tuppence realized that the dirty and worn books had been
replaced by new and cleaner editions and was rather amused.
Mrs. Sprot was very much what Tuppence thought of as
"the hygienic mother." Always terrified of germs, of impure
food, or of the child suckling a soiled toy.

Tuppence, brought up in a free and easy Rectory life, was
always rather contemptuous of exaggerated hygiene and had
brought up her own two children to absorb what she called
a "reasonable amount" of dirt. However, she obediently took
out the clean copy of Jack Horner and read it to the child
with the comments proper to the occasion. Betty murmuring,
"That's Jack!—Plum!—In a *Pie,"* pointing out these interesting objects with a sticky finger that bade fair to soon
consign this second copy to the scrap heap. They proceeded
to *Goosey Goosey Gander* and the *Old Woman Who Lived
in a Shoe,* and then Betty hid the books and Tuppence took
an amazingly long time to find each of them, to Betty's
great glee, and so the morning passed rapidly away.

After lunch Betty had her rest and it was then that Mrs.
O'Rourke invited Tuppence into her room.

Mrs. O'Rourke's room was very untidy and smelled
strongly of peppermint and stale cake, with a faint odour
of moth balls added. There were photographs on every
table of Mrs. O'Rourke's children and grandchildren and
nieces and nephews and great nieces and great nephews.
There were so many of them that Tuppence felt as though
she were looking at a realistically produced play of the late
Victorian period.

" 'Tis a grand way you have with children, Mrs. Blenkensop," observed Mrs. O'Rourke genially.

"Oh, well," said Tuppence, "with my own two—"

Mrs. O'Rourke cut in quickly:

"Two? It was three boys I understood you had?"

"Oh, yes, three. But two of them are very near in age and

I was thinking of the days spent with them."

"Ah! I see. Sit down now, Mrs. Blenkensop. Make yourself at home."

Tuppence sat down obediently and wished that Mrs. O'Rourke did not always make her feel so uncomfortable. She felt now exactly like Hansel or Gretel accepting the witch's invitation.

"Tell me now," said Mrs. O'Rourke. "What do you think of Sans Souci?"

Tuppence began a somewhat gushing speech of eulogy, but Mrs. O'Rourke cut her short without ceremony.

"What I'd be asking you is if you don't feel there's something odd about the place?"

"Odd? No, I don't think so."

"Not about Mrs. Perenna? You're interested in her, you must allow. I've seen you watching her and watching her."

Tuppence flushed.

"She—she's an interesting woman."

"She is not then," said Mrs. O'Rourke. "She's a commonplace woman enough—that is if she's what she seems. But perhaps she isn't. Is that your idea?"

"Really, Mrs. O'Rourke, I don't know *what* you mean."

"Have you ever stopped to think that many of us are that way—different to what we seem on the surface. Mr. Meadowes, now. He's a puzzling kind of man. Sometimes I'd say he was a typical Englishman, stupid to the core, and there's other times I'll catch a look or a word that's not stupid at all. It's odd that, don't you think so?"

Tuppence said firmly:

"Oh, I really think Mr. Meadowes is *very* typical."

"There are others. Perhaps you'll know who I'll be meaning?"

Tuppence shook her head.

"The name," said Mrs. O'Rourke encouragingly, "begins with an S."

She nodded her head several times.

With a sudden spark of anger and an obscure impulse to spring to the defense of something young and vulnerable, Tuppence said sharply:

"Sheila's just a rebel. One usually is, at that age."

Mrs. O'Rourke nodded her head several times, looking just like an obese china mandarin that Tuppence remembered on her Aunt Gracie's mantelpiece. A vast smile tilted up the corners of her mouth. She said softly:

"You mayn't know it, but Miss Minton's Christian name is Sophia."

"Oh!" Tuppence was taken aback. "Was it Miss Minton you meant?"

"It was not," said Mrs. O'Rourke.

Tuppence turned away to the window. Queer how this old woman could affect her, spreading about her an atmosphere of unrest and fear. "Like a mouse between a cat's paws," thought Tuppence. "That's what I feel like . . ."

This vast smiling monumental old woman, sitting there, almost purring—and yet there was the pat-pat of paws playing with something that wasn't, in spite of the purring, to be allowed to get away . . .

Nonsense—all nonsense! I imagine these things, thought Tuppence, staring out of the window into the garden. The rain had stopped. There was a gentle patter of raindrops off the trees.

Tuppence thought: "It isn't all my fancy. I'm not a fanciful person. There is something, some focus of evil here. If I could see—"

Her thoughts broke off abruptly.

At the bottom of the garden the bushes parted slightly. In the gap a face appeared, staring stealthily up at the house. It was the face of the foreign woman who had stood talking to Carl von Deinim in the road.

It was so still, so unblinking in its regard, that it seemed to Tuppence as though it was not human. Staring, staring up at the windows of Sans Souci. It was devoid of expression, and yet there was—yes, undoubtedly there was, menace about it. Immobile, implacable. It represented some spirit, some force, alien to Sans Souci and the commonplace banality of English guest house life. So, Tuppence thought, might Jael have looked, waiting to drive the nail through the forehead of sleeping Sisera.

These thoughts took only a second or two to flash through Tuppence's mind. Turning abruptly from the window, she murmured something to Mrs. O'Rourke, hurried out of the room and ran down stairs and out of the front door.

Turning to the right, she ran down the side garden path to where she had seen the face. There was no one there now. Tuppence went through the shrubbery and out on to the road and looked up and down the hill. She could see no one. Where had the woman gone?

Vexed, she turned and went back into the grounds of Sans Souci. Could she have imagined the whole thing? No, the woman had been there.

Obstinately she wandered round the garden, peering behind bushes. She got very wet and found no trace of the strange woman. She retraced her steps to the house with a vague feeling of foreboding—a queer formless dread of something about to happen.

She did not guess, would never have guessed, what that something was going to be.

TWO

Now that the weather had cleared, Miss Minton was dressing Betty preparatory to taking her out for a walk. They were going down to the town to buy a celluloid duck to sail in Betty's bath.

Betty was very excited and capered so violently that it was extremely difficult to insert her arms into the woolly pullover. The two set off together, Betty chattering violently: "Byaduck, Byaduck. For Bettibarf. For Bettibarf," and deriving great pleasure from a ceaseless reiteration of these important facts.

Two matches, left carelessly crossed on the marble table in the hall, informed Tuppence that Mr. Meadowes was spending the afternoon on the trail of Mrs. Perenna. Tuppence betook herself to the drawing room and the company of Mr. and Mrs. Cayley.

Mr. Cayley was in a fretful mood. He had come to Leahampton, he explained, for absolute rest and quiet, and what quiet could there be with a child in the house? All day long it went on, screaming and running about, jumping up and down on the floors—

His wife murmured pacifically that Betty was really a dear little mite, but the remark met with no favour.

"No doubt, no doubt," said Mr. Cayley, wriggling his long neck. "But her mother should keep her quiet. There are other people to consider. Invalids, people whose nerves need repose."

Tuppence said: "It's not easy to keep a child of that age quiet. It's not natural—there would be something wrong with the child if she was quiet."

Mr. Cayley gobbled angrily:

"Nonsense—nonsense—this foolish modern spirit. Letting children do exactly as they please. A child should be made to sit down quietly and—and nurse a doll—or read, or something."

"She's not three yet," said Tuppence, smiling. "You can hardly expect her to be able to read."

"Well, something must be done about it. I shall speak to Mrs. Perenna. The child was singing, singing in her bed before seven o'clock this morning. I had had a bad night and just dropped off towards morning—and it woke me right up."

"It's very important that Mr. Cayley should get as much sleep as possible," said Mrs. Cayley anxiously. "The doctor said so."

"You should go to a nursing home," said Tuppence.

"My dear lady, such places are ruinously expensive and besides it's not the right atmosphere. There is a suggestion of illness that reacts unfavourably on my sub-conscious."

"Bright society, the doctor said," Mrs. Cayley explained helpfully. "A normal life. He thought a guest house would be better than just taking a furnished house. Mr. Cayley would not be so likely to brood, and would be stimulated by exchanging ideas with other people."

Mr. Cayley's method of exchanging ideas was, so far as Tuppence could judge, a mere recital of his own ailments and symptoms and the exchange consisted in the sympathetic or unsympathetic reception of them.

Adroitly, Tuppence changed the subject.

"I wish you would tell me," she said, "of your own views on life in Germany. You told me you had travelled there a good deal in recent years. It would be interesting to have the point of view of an experienced man of the world like yourself. I can see you are the kind of man, quite unswayed by prejudice, who could really give a clear account of conditions there."

Flattery, in Tuppence's opinion, should always be laid on with a trowel where a man was concerned. Mr. Cayley rose at once to the bait.

"As you say, dear lady, I am capable of taking a clear unprejudiced view. Now, in my opinion—"

What followed constituted a monologue. Tuppence, throwing in an occasional "Now that's very interesting" or "What a shrewd observer you are," listened with an attention that was not assumed for the occasion. For Mr. Cayley, carried away by the sympathy of his listener, was displaying himself as a decided admirer of the Nazi system. How much better it would have been, he hinted, if he did not say, for England and Germany to have allied themselves against the rest of Europe.

The return of Miss Minton and Betty, the celluloid duck duly obtained, broke in upon the monologue, which had extended unbroken for nearly two hours. Looking up, Tuppence caught rather a curious expression on Mrs. Cayley's face. She found it hard to define. It might be merely pardonable wifely jealousy at the monopoly of her husband's attention by another woman. It might be alarm at the fact that Mr. Cayley was being too outspoken in his political views. It certainly expressed dissatisfaction.

Tea was the next move and hard on that came the return of Mrs. Sprot from London, exclaiming:

"I do hope Betty's been good and not troublesome? Have you been a good girl, Betty?" To which Betty replied laconically by the single word:

"Dam!"

This, however, was not to be regarded as an expression of disapproval at her mother's return, but merely as a request for blackberry preserve.

It elicited a deep chuckle from Mrs. O'Rourke and a reproachful:

"Please, Betty, dear," from the young lady's parent.

Mrs. Sprot then sat down, drank several cups of tea, and plunged into a spirited narrative of her purchases in London, the crowd on the train, what a soldier recently returned from France had told the occupants of her carriage, and what a girl behind the stocking counter had told her of a recent air raid in one of the suburbs.

The conversation was, in fact, completely normal. It was prolonged afterwards on the terrace outside, for the sun was now shining and the wet day a thing of the past.

Betty rushed happily about, making mysterious expeditions into the bushes and returning with a laurel leaf, or a heap of pebbles which she placed in the lap of one of the grown-ups with a confused and unintelligible explanation of what it represented. Fortunately she required little co-operation in her game, being satisfied with an occasional "How nice, darling. Is it really?"

Never had there been an evening more typical of Sans Souci at its most harmless. Chatter, gossip, speculations as to the course of the war—can France rally? Will Weygand pull things together? What is Russia likely to do? Could Hitler invade England if he tried? Will Paris fall if the "bulge" is not straightened out? Was it true that . . . ? It had been said that . . . And it was rumoured that . . .

Political and military scandal was happily bandied about.

Tuppence thought to herself: "Chatterbugs a danger? Nonsense, they're a safety valve. People *enjoy* these rumours. It gives them the stimulation to carry on with their own private worries and anxieties." She contributed a nice tidbit prefixed by, "My son told me—of course this is *quite* private, you understand—"

Suddenly, with a start, Mrs. Sprot glanced at her watch.

"Goodness, it's nearly seven. I ought to have put that child to bed hours ago. Betty—Betty!"

It was some time since Betty had returned to the terrace, though no one had noticed her defection.

Mrs. Sprot called her with rising impatience.

"Bett-eeee! Where can the child be?"

Mrs. O'Rourke said, with her deep laugh:

"Up to mischief, I've no doubt of it. 'Tis always the way when there's peace."

"Betty! I want you."

There was no answer and Mrs. Sprot rose impatiently.

"I suppose I must go and look for her. I wonder where she can be?"

Miss Minton suggested that she was hiding somewhere and Tuppence, with memories of her own childhood, suggested the kitchen. But Betty could not be found, either inside or outside the house. They went round the garden calling, looking all over the bedrooms. There was no Betty anywhere.

Mrs. Sprot began to get annoyed.

"It's very naughty of her—very naughty indeed! Do you think she can have gone out on the road?"

Together she and Tuppence went out to the gate and looked up and down the hill. There was no one in sight except a tradesman's boy with a bicycle standing talking to a maid at the door of St. Lucian's opposite.

On Tuppence's suggestion, she and Mrs. Sprot crossed the road and the latter asked if either of them had noticed a little girl. They both shook their heads and then the servant asked, with sudden recollection:

"A little girl in a green checked gingham dress?"

Mrs. Sprot said eagerly:

"That's right."

"I saw her about half an hour ago—going down the road with a woman."

Mrs. Sprot said, with astonishment:

"With a woman? What sort of a woman?"

The girl seemed slightly embarrassed.

"Well, what I'd call an odd looking kind of woman. A foreigner she was. Queer clothes. A kind of shawl thing and no hat, and a strange sort of face—queer like, if you know what I mean. I've seen her about once or twice lately, and to tell the truth I thought she was a bit wanting—If you know what I mean," she added helpfully.

In a flash Tuppence remembered the face she had seen that afternoon peering through the bushes and the foreboding that had swept over her.

But she had never thought of the woman in connection with the child, could not understand it now.

She had little time for meditation, however. Mrs. Sprot almost collapsed against her.

"Oh, Betty, my little girl. She's been kidnapped. She—what did the woman look like—a gypsy?"

Tuppence shook her head energetically.

"No, she was fair, very fair, a broad face with high cheek bones and blue eyes set very far apart."

She saw Mrs. Sprot staring at her and hastened to explain.

"I saw the woman this afternoon—peering through the bushes at the bottom of the garden. And I've noticed her hanging about. Carl von Deinim was speaking to her one day. It must be the same woman."

The servant girl chimed in to say:

"That's right. Fair-haired, she was. And wanting, if you ask me. Didn't understand nothing that was said to her."

"Oh, God," moaned Mrs. Sprot. "What shall I do?"

Tuppence passed an arm round her.

"Come back to the house, have a little brandy and then we'll ring up the police. It's all right. We'll get her back."

Mrs. Sprot went with her meekly, murmuring in a dazed fashion:

"I can't imagine how Betty would go like that with a stranger."

"She's very young," said Tuppence. "Not old enough to be shy."

Mrs. Sprot cried out weakly:

"Some dreadful German woman, I expect. She'll kill my Betty."

"Nonsense," said Tuppence robustly. "It will be all right. I expect she's just some woman who's not quite right in her head." But she did not believe her own words—did not believe for one moment that that calm blond woman was an irresponsible lunatic.

Carl! Would Carl know? Had Carl something to do with this?

A few minutes later she was inclined to doubt this. Carl von Deinim, like the rest, seemed amazed, unbelieving, completely surprised.

As soon as the facts were made plain, Major Bletchley assumed control.

"Now then, dear lady," he said to Mrs. Sprot, "sit down here—just drink a little drop of this—brandy—it won't hurt you—and I'll get straight on to the police station."

Mrs. Sprot murmured:

"Wait a minute—there might be something—"

She hurried up the stairs and along the passage to hers and Betty's room.

A minute or two later they heard her footsteps running wildly along the landing. She rushed down the stairs like a demented woman and clutched Major Bletchley's hand from the telephone receiver, which he was just about to lift.

"No, no," she panted. "You mustn't—you mustn't . . ."

And sobbing wildly, she collapsed into a chair.

They crowded around her. In a minute or two, she recovered her composure. Sitting up, with Mrs. Cayley's arm round her, she held something out for them to see.

"I found this—on the floor of my room. It had been wrapped round a stone and thrown through the window. Look—look what it says."

Tommy took it from her and unfolded it.

It was a note, written in a queer stiff foreign handwriting, big and bold.

WE HAVE GOT YOUR CHILD IN SAFE KEEP-
ING. YOU WILL BE TOLD WHAT TO DO IN DUE
COURSE. IF YOU GO TO THE POLICE YOUR
CHILD WILL BE KILLED. SAY NOTHING. WAIT
FOR INSTRUCTIONS. IF NOT— X.

Mrs. Sprot was moaning faintly:

"Betty—Betty—"

Everyone was talking at once. "The dirty murdering scoundrels!" from Mrs. O'Rourke. "Brutes!" from Sheila Perenna. "Fantastic, fantastic—I don't believe a word of it. Silly practical joke," from Mr. Cayley. "Oh, the dear, wee mite," from Miss Minton. "I do not understand. It is incredible," from Carl von Deinim. And above everyone else the strenuous voice of Major Bletchley:

"Damned nonsense. Intimidation. We must inform the police at once. They'll soon get to the bottom of it."

Once more he moved towards the telephone. This time a scream of outraged motherhood from Mrs. Sprot stopped him.

He shouted:

"But, my dear Madam, it's *got* to be done. This is only a crude device to prevent you getting on the track of these scoundrels."

"They'll kill her."

"Nonsense. They wouldn't dare."

"I won't have it, I tell you. I'm her mother. It's for me to say."

"I know. I know. That's what they're counting on—your feeling like that. Very natural. But you must take it from me, a soldier and an experienced man of the world, the police are what we need."

"No!"

Bletchley's eyes went round seeking allies.

"Meadowes, you agree with me?"

Slowly, Tommy nodded.

"Cayley? Look, Mrs. Sprot, both Meadowes and Cayley agree."

Mrs. Sprot said, with sudden energy:

"Men! All of you! Ask the women!"

Tommy's eyes sought Tuppence. Tuppence said, her voice low and shaken:

"I—I agree with Mrs. Sprot."

She was thinking, "Deborah! Derek! If it were them. I'd feel like her. Tommy and the others are right, I've no doubt, but all the same I couldn't do it. I couldn't risk it."

Mrs. O'Rourke was saying:

"No mother alive could risk it and that's a fact."

Mrs. Cayley murmured:

"I do think, you know, that—well—" and trailed off into incoherence.

Miss Minton said tremulously:

"Such awful things happen. We'd never forgive ourselves if anything happened to dear little Betty."

Tuppence said sharply:

"You haven't said anything, Mr. von Deinim?"

Carl's blue eyes were very bright. His face was a mask. He said slowly and stiffly:

"I am a foreigner. I do not know your English police. How competent they are—how quick."

Someone had come in to the hall. It was Mrs. Perenna; her cheeks were flushed. Evidently she had been hurrying up the hill. She said:

"What's all this?" And her voice was commanding, imperious, not the complaisant guest house hostess, but a woman of force.

They told her—a confused tale told by too many people, but she grasped it quickly.

And with her grasping of it, the whole thing seemed, in a way, to be passed up to her for judgment. She was the supreme court.

She held the hastily scrawled note a minute, then she handed it back. Her words came sharp and authoritative.

"The police? They'll be no good. You can't risk their blundering. Take the law into your own hands. Go after the child yourself."

Bletchley said, shrugging his shoulders:

"Very well. If you won't call in the police, it's the best thing to be done."

Tommy said:

"They can't have got much of a start."

"Half an hour, the maid said," Tuppence put in.

"Haydock," said Bletchley. "Haydock's the man to help us. He's got a car. The woman's unusual looking, you say? And a foreigner? Ought to leave a trail that we can follow. Come on, there's no time to be lost. You'll come along, Meadowes?"

Mrs. Sprot got up.

"I'm coming, too."

"Now, my dear lady, leave it to us—"

"I'm coming, too."

"Oh, well—"

He gave in—murmuring something about the female of the species being deadlier than the male.

THREE

In the end Commander Haydock, taking in the situation with commendable Naval rapidity, drove the car. Tommy sat beside him, and behind were Bletchley, Mrs. Sprot and Tuppence. Not only did Mrs. Sprot cling to her, but Tuppence was the only one (with the exception of Carl von Deinim) who knew the mysterious kidnapper by sight.

The Commander was a good organizer and a quick worker. In next to no time, he had filled up the car with petrol, tossed a map of the district and a larger scale map of Leahampton itself to Bletchley and was ready to start off.

Mrs. Sprot had run upstairs again, presumably to her room to get a coat. But when she got into the car and they had started down the hill she disclosed to Tuppence something in her handbag. It was a small pistol.

She said quietly:

"I got it from Major Bletchley's room. I remember his mentioning one day that he had one."

Tuppence looked a little dubious.

"You don't think that—"

Mrs. Sprot said, her mouth a thin line:

"It may come in useful."

Tuppence sat marvelling at the strange forces maternity will set loose in an ordinary, commonplace young woman. She could visualize Mrs. Sprot, the kind of woman who would normally declare herself frightened to death of fire-arms, coolly shooting down any person who had harmed her child.

They drove first, on the Commander's suggestion, to the railway station. A train had left Leahampton about twenty minutes earlier and it was possible that the fugitives had gone by it.

At the station they separated, the Commander taking the ticket collector, Tommy the booking office, and Bletchley the porters outside. Tuppence and Mrs. Sprot went into the Ladies' Room on the chance that the woman had gone in there to change her appearance before taking the train.

One and all drew blank. It was now more difficult to

shape a course. In all probability, as Haydock pointed out, the kidnappers had had a car waiting, and once Betty had been persuaded to come away with the woman, they had made their getaway in that. It was here, as Bletchley pointed out once more, that the co-operation of the police was so vital. It needed an organization of that kind who could send out messages all over the country, covering the different roads.

Mrs. Sprot merely shook her head, her lips pressed tightly together.

Tuppence said:

"We must put ourselves in their places. Where would they have waited in the car? Somewhere as near Sans Souci as possible, but where a car wouldn't be noticed. Now let's *think*. The woman and Betty walk down the hill together. At the bottom is the esplanade. The car might have been drawn up there. So long as you don't leave it unattended you can stop there for quite a while. The only other places are the Car Park in James Square, also quite near, or else one of the small streets that lead off from the esplanade."

It was at that moment that a small man, with a diffident manner and pince-nez, stepped up to them and said, stammering a little:

"Excuse me. . . . No offense, I hope . . . but I c-c-couldn't help overhearing what you were asking the porter just now." (He now directed his remarks to Major Bletchley.) "I was not listening, of course; just came down to see about a parcel—extraordinary how long things are delayed just now—movements of troops, they say—but really most difficult when it's perishable—the parcel, I mean —and so, you see, I happened to overhear—and really it did seem the most wonderful coincidence . . ."

Mrs. Sprot sprang forward. She seized him by the arm.

"You've seen her? You've seen my little girl?"

"Oh, really, your little girl, you say? Now fancy that—"

Mrs. Sprot cried: "Tell me." And her fingers bit into the little man's arm so that he winced.

Tuppence said quickly:

"Please tell us anything you have seen as quickly as you can. We shall be most grateful if you will."

"Oh, well, really, of course, it may be nothing at all. But the description fitted so well—"

Tuppence felt the woman beside her trembling, but she herself strove to keep her manner calm and unhurried. She knew the type with which they were dealing—fussy, muddle-headed, diffident, incapable of going straight to the point and worse if hurried. She said:

"Please tell us."

"It was only—my name is Robbins, by the way, Edward Robbins—"

"Yes, Mr. Robbins."

"I live at Whiteways, in Ernes Cliff Road, one of those new houses on the new road—most labour saving, and really *every* convenience, and a beautiful view and the downs only a stone's throw away."

With a glance Tuppence quelled Major Bletchley, who she saw was about to break out, and she said:

"And you saw the little girl we are looking for?"

"Yes, I really think it *must* be. A little girl with a foreign looking woman, you said? It was really the woman I noticed. Because, of course, we are all on the lookout nowadays for Fifth Columnists, aren't we? A sharp lookout, that is what they say, and I always try to do so, and so, as I say, I noticed the woman. A nurse, I thought, or a maid—a lot of spies came over here in that capacity, and this woman was most unusual looking and walking up the road and on to the downs—with a little girl—and the little girl seemed tired and rather lagging, and half past seven, well, most children go to bed then, so I looked at the woman pretty sharply. I think it flustered her. She hurried to the road, pulling the child after her, and finally picked her up and went on up the path out on to the cliff, which I thought *strange*, you know, because there are no houses there at all—nothing—not until you get to Whitehaven—about five miles over the downs— a favourite walk for hikers. But in this case I thought it odd. I wondered if the woman was going to signal, perhaps. One hears of so much enemy activity and she certainly looked uneasy when she saw me staring at her."

Commander Haydock was back in the car and had started the engine. He said:

"Ernes Cliff Road, you say? That's right the other side of the town, isn't it?"

"Yes, you go along the esplanade and past the old town and then up—"

The others had jumped in, not listening further to Mr. Robbins.

Tuppence called out:

"Thank you, Mr. Robbins," and they drove off leaving him staring after them with his mouth open.

They drove rapidly through the town, avoiding accidents more by good luck than by skill. But the luck held. They came out at last at a mass of straggling building development, somewhat marred by proximity to the gas works. A series of little roads led up towards the downs, stopping abruptly a short way up the hill. Ernes Cliff Road was the third of these.

Commander Haydock turned smartly into it and drove up. At the end the road petered out on to bare hillside up which a footpath meandered.

"Better get out and walk here," said Bletchley.

Haydock said dubiously:

"Could almost take the car up. Ground's firm enough. Bit bumpy but I think she could do it."

Mrs. Sprot cried:

"Oh, yes, please, please. . . . We must be quick."

The Commander murmured to himself.

"Hope to goodness we're after the right lot. That little pip-squeak may have seen any woman with a kid."

The car groaned uneasily as she ploughed her way up over the rough ground. The gradient was severe, but the turf was short and springy. They came out without mishap on the top of the rise. Here the view was less interrupted till it rested in the distance on the curve of Whitehaven Bay.

Bletchley said:

"Not a bad idea. The woman could spend the night up here if need be, drop down into Whitehaven tomorrow morning and take a train there."

Haydock said:

"No signs of them as far as I can see."

He was standing up holding to his eyes some field glasses

that he had thoughtfully brought with him. Suddenly his figure became tense as he focussed the glasses on two small moving dots.

"Got 'em, by Jove. . . ."

He dropped into the driver's seat again and the car bucketed forward. The chase was a short one now. Shot up in the air, tossed from side to side, the occupants of the car gained rapidly on those two small dots. They could be distinguished now—a tall figure and a short one—nearer still, a woman holding a child by the hand—still nearer, yes, a child in a green gingham frock. Betty.

Mrs. Sprot gave a strangled cry.

"All right now, my dear," said Major Bletchley, patting her kindly. "We've got 'em."

They went on. Suddenly the woman turned and saw the car advancing towards her.

With a cry she caught up the child in her arms and began running.

She ran, not forward, but sideways towards the edge of the cliff.

The car, after a few yards, could not follow, the ground was too uneven and blocked with big boulders. It stopped and the occupants tumbled out.

Mrs. Sprot was out first and running wildly after the two fugitives.

The others followed her.

When they were within twenty yards, the other woman turned at bay. She was standing now at the very edge of the cliff. With a hoarse cry she clutched the child closer.

Haydock cried out:

"My God, she's going to throw the kid over the cliff. . . ."

The woman stood there, clutching Betty tightly. Her face was disfigured with a frenzy of hate. She uttered a long hoarse sentence that none of them understood. And still she held the child and looked from time to time at the drop below—not a yard from where she stood.

It seemed clear that she was threatening to throw the child over the cliff.

All of them stood there, dazed, terrified, unable to move for fear of precipitating a catastrophe.

Haydock was tugging at his pocket. He pulled out a service revolver.

He shouted:

"Put that child down—or I fire."

The foreign woman laughed. She held the child closer to her breast. The two figures were moulded into one.

Haydock muttered:

"I daren't shoot. I'd hit the child."

Tommy said:

"The woman's crazy. She'll jump over with the child in another moment."

Haydock said again, helplessly:

"I daren't shoot—"

But at that moment a shot rang out. The woman swayed and fell, the child still clasped in her arms.

The men ran forward. Mrs. Sprot stood swaying, the smoking pistol in her hand, her eyes dilated.

She took a few stiff steps forward.

Tommy was kneeling by the bodies. He turned them gently. He saw the woman's face—noted appreciatively its strange wild beauty. The eyes opened, looked at him, then went blank. With a little sigh, the woman died, shot through the head.

Unhurt, little Betty Sprot wriggled out and ran towards her mother who was standing like a statue.

Then, at last, Mrs. Sprot crumpled. She flung away the pistol and dropped down, clutching the child to her.

She cried:

"She's safe—she's safe—Oh, Betty—*Betty*." And then, in a low, awed whisper:

"Did I—did I—kill her?"

Tuppence said firmly:

"Don't think about it—don't think about it. Think about Betty. Just think about Betty."

Mrs. Sprot held the child close against her, sobbing.

Tuppence went forward to join the men.

Haydock murmured:

"Bloody miracle. I couldn't have brought off a shot like that. Don't believe the woman's ever handled a pistol before either—sheer instinct. A miracle, that's what it is."

Tuppence said:

"Thank God! It was a near thing!" And she looked down at the sheer drop to the sea below and shuddered.

8

It was not until some days later that Mrs. Blenkensop and Mr. Meadowes were able to meet and compare notes.

The intervening days had been busy. The dead woman had been identified as Vanda Polonska, a Polish refugee who had entered the country soon after the outbreak of war. Very little was known about her, but she appeared to have received certain sums of money from an unknown source which pointed to the probability of her being an enemy agent of some kind.

"And so it's a blank wall as usual," said Tommy gloomily.

Tuppence nodded.

"Yes, they seal up both ends, don't they? No papers, no hints of any kind as to who she had dealings with."

"Too damned efficient," said Tommy.

He added:

"You know, Tuppence, I don't like the look of things."

Tuppence assented. The news was indeed far from reassuring.

The French Army was in retreat and it seemed doubtful if the tide could be turned. Evacuation from Dunkerque was in progress. It was clearly a matter of a few days only before Paris fell. There was a general dismay at the revelation of lack of equipment and of material for resisting the Germans' great mechanized units.

Tommy said:

"Is it only our usual muddling and slowness? Or has there been deliberate engineering behind this?"

"The latter, I think, but they'll never be able to prove it."

"No. Our adversaries are too darned clever for that."

"We are combing out a lot of the rot now."

"Oh, yes, we're rounding up the obvious people, but I don't believe we've got at the brains that are behind it all. Brains, organization, a whole carefully thought-out plan—a plan which uses our habits of dilatoriness, and our petty feuds, and our slowness for its own ends."

Tuppence said:

"That's what we're here for—and we haven't got results."

"We've done something," Tommy reminded her.

"Carl von Deinim and Vanda Polonska, yes. The small fry."

"You think they were working together?"

"I think they must have been," said Tuppence thoughtfully. "Remember, I saw them talking."

"Then Carl von Deinim must have engineered the kidnapping."

"I suppose so."

"But why?"

"I don't know," said Tuppence. "That's what I keep thinking and thinking about. It doesn't make sense."

"Why kidnap that particular child? Who are the Sprots? They've no money—so it isn't ransom. They're neither of them employed by the Government in any capacity."

"I know, Tommy. It just doesn't make any sense at all."

"Hasn't Mrs. Sprot any idea herself?"

"That woman," said Tuppence scornfully, "hasn't got the brains of a hen. She doesn't think at all. Just says it's the sort of thing the wicked Germans would do."

"Silly ass," said Tommy. "The Germans are efficient. If they send one of their agents to kidnap a brat, it's for some reason."

"I've a feeling, you know," said Tuppence, "that Mrs. Sprot could get at the reason if only she'd think about it. There must be something—some piece of information that she herself has inadvertently got hold of, perhaps without knowing what it is exactly."

"*Say nothing. Wait for instructions.*" Tommy quoted from

the note found on Mrs. Sprot's bedroom floor. "Damn it all, that means something."

"Of course it does—it must. The only thing I can think of is that Mrs. Sprot, or her husband, has been given something to keep by someone else—given it, perhaps, just because they are such humdrum ordinary people that no one would suspect they had it—whatever 'it' may be."

"It's an idea, that."

"I know—but it's awfully like a spy story. It doesn't seem real somehow."

"Have you asked Mrs. Sprot to rack her brains a bit?"

"Yes, the trouble is that she isn't really interested. All she cares about is getting Betty back—that, and having hysterics because she's shot someone."

"Funny creatures, women," mused Tommy. "There was that woman, went out that day like an avenging fury, she'd have shot down a regiment in cold blood without turning a hair just to get her child back, and then, having shot the kidnapper by a perfectly incredible fluke, she breaks down and comes all over squeamish about it."

"The coroner exonerated her all right," said Tuppence.

"Naturally. By Jove, I wouldn't have risked firing when she did."

Tuppence said:

"No more would she, probably, if she'd known more about it. It was sheer ignorance of the difficulty of the shot that made her bring it off."

Tommy nodded.

"Quite Biblical," he said. "David and Goliath."

"Oh!" said Tuppence.

"What is it, old thing?"

"I don't quite know. When you said that something twanged somewhere in my brain, and now it's gone again!"

"Very useful," said Tommy.

"Don't be scathing. That sort of thing does happen sometimes."

"Gentleman who drew a bow at a venture, was that it?"

"No, it was—wait a minute—I think it was something to do with Solomon."

"Cedars, temples, a lot of wives and concubines?"

"Stop," said Tuppence, putting her hands to her ears.
"You're making it worse."

"Jews?" said Tommy hopefully. "Tribes of Israel?"

But Tuppence shook her head. After a minute or two
she said:

"I wish I could remember who it was that woman reminded me of."

"The late Vanda Polonska?"

"Yes. The first time I saw her her face seemed vaguely
familiar."

"Do you think you had come across her somewhere else?"

"No, I'm sure I hadn't."

"Mrs. Perenna and Sheila are a totally different type."

"Oh, yes, it wasn't them. You know, Tommy, about
those two. I've been thinking."

"To any good purpose?"

"I'm not sure. It's about that note—the one Mrs. Sprot
found on the floor in her room when Betty was kidnapped."

"Well?"

"All that about its being wrapped round a stone and
thrown through the window is rubbish. It was put there by
someone—ready for Mrs. Sprot to find—and I think it was
Mrs. Perenna who put it there."

"Mrs. Perenna, Carl, Vanda Poloska—all working
together."

"Yes. Did you notice how Mrs. Perenna came in just at
the critical moment and clinched things—not to ring up the
police? She took command of the whole situation."

"So she's still your selection for M?"

"Yes, isn't she yours?"

"I suppose so," said Tommy slowly.

"Why, Tommy, have you got another idea?"

"It's probably an awfully dud one."

"Tell me."

"No, I'd rather not. I've nothing to go on. Nothing whatever. But if I'm right, it's not M we're up against, but N."

He thought to himself:

"Bletchley. I suppose he's all right. Why shouldn't he be?

He's a true enough type—almost too true, and after all, it was he who wanted to ring up the police. Yes, but he could have been pretty sure that the child's mother wouldn't stand for the idea. The threatening note made sure of that. He could afford to urge the opposite point of view—"

And that brought him back again to the vexing, teasing problem to which as yet he could find no answer.

Why kidnap Betty Sprot?

TWO

There was a car standing outside Sans Souci bearing the word POLICE on it.

Absorbed in her own thoughts Tuppence took little notice of that. She turned in at the drive and entering the front door went straight upstairs to her own room.

She stopped, taken aback, on the threshold, as a tall figure turned away from the window.

"Dear me," said Tuppence. "Sheila?"

The girl came straight towards her. Now Tuppence saw her more clearly, saw the blazing eyes deep set in the white tragic face.

Sheila said:

"I'm glad you've come. I've been waiting for you."

"What's the matter?"

The girl's voice was quiet and devoid of emotion. She said:

"They have arrested Carl!"

"The police?"

"Yes."

"Oh, dear," said Tuppence. She felt inadequate to the situation. Quiet as Sheila's voice had been, Tuppence was under no misapprehension as to what lay behind it.

Whether they were fellow conspirators or not, this girl loved Carl von Deinim, and Tuppence felt her heart aching in sympathy with this tragic young creature.

Sheila said:

"What shall I do?"

The simple forlorn question made Tuppence wince. She said helplessly:

"Oh, my dear."

Sheila said, and her voice was like a mourning harp:

"They've taken him away. I shall never see him again."

She cried out:

"What shall I do? What shall I do?" And flinging herself down on her knees by the bed, she wept her heart out.

Tuppence stroked the dark head. She said presently, in a weak voice:

"It—it may not be true. Perhaps they are only going to intern him. After all, he is an enemy alien, you know."

"That's not what they said. They're searching his room now."

Tuppence said slowly, "Well, if they find nothing—"

"They will find nothing, of course! What should they find?"

"I don't know. I thought perhaps you might?"

"I?"

Her scorn, her amazement were too real to be feigned. Any suspicions Tuppence had had that Sheila Perenna was involved died at this moment. The girl knew nothing, had never known anything.

Tuppence said:

"If he is innocent—"

Sheila interrupted her.

"What does that matter? The police will make a case against him."

Tuppence said sharply:

"Nonsense, my dear child, that really isn't true."

"The English police will do anything. My Mother says so."

"Your Mother may say so, but she's wrong. I assure you that it isn't so."

Sheila looked at her doubtfully for a minute or two. Then she said:

"Very well. If you say so. I trust you."

Tuppence felt very uncomfortable. She said sharply:

"You trust too much, Sheila. You may have been unwise to trust Carl."

"Are you against him, too? I thought you liked him. He thinks so, too."

Touching young things—with their faith in one's liking for them. And it was true—she had liked Carl—she did like him.

Rather wearily she said:

"Listen, Sheila, liking or not liking has nothing to do with facts. This country and Germany are at war. There are many ways of serving one's country. One of them is to get information—and to work behind the lines. It is a brave thing to do, for when you are caught, it is"—her voice broke a little—"the end."

Sheila said:

"You think Carl—"

"Might be working for his country that way? It is a possibility, isn't it?"

"No," said Sheila.

"It would be his job, you see, to come over here as a refugee, to appear to be violently anti-Nazi and then to gather information."

Sheila said quietly:

"It's not true. I know Carl. I know his heart and his mind. He cares most for science—for his work—for the truth and the knowledge in it. He is grateful to England for letting him work here. Sometimes, when people say cruel things, he feels German and bitter. But he hates the Nazis always and what they stand for—their denial of freedom."

Tuppence said:

"He would say so, of course."

Sheila turned reproachful eyes upon her.

"So you believe he is a spy?"

"I think it is"—Tuppence hesitated—"a possibility."

Sheila walked to the door.

"I see. I'm sorry I came to ask you to help us."

"But what did you think I could do, dear child?"

"You know people. Your sons are in the Army and Navy and I've heard you say more than once that they knew influential people. I thought perhaps you could get them to—to do—something?"

Tuppence thought of those mythical creatures, Douglas and Raymond and Cyril.

"I'm afraid," she said, "that they couldn't do anything."

Sheila flung her head up. She said passionately:

"Then there's no hope for us. They'll take him away and shut him up, and one day, early in the morning, they'll stand him against a wall and shoot him—and that will be the end."

She went out, shutting the door behind her.

"Oh, damn, damn, damn the Irish!" thought Tuppence in a fury of mixed feelings. "Why have they got that terrible power of twisting things until you don't know where you are? If Carl von Deinim's a spy, he deserves to be shot. I must hang on to that, not let that girl with her Irish voice bewitch me into thinking it's the tragedy of a hero and a martyr!"

She recalled the voice of a famous actress speaking a line from *Riders to the Sea.*

"It's the fine quiet time they'll be having. . . ."

Poignant . . . carrying you away on a tide of feeling . . .

She thought, "If it weren't true. Oh, if only it weren't true. . . ."

Yet, knowing what she did, how could she doubt?

THREE

The fisherman on the end of the Old Pier cast in his line and then reeled it cautiously in.

"No doubt whatever, I'm afraid," he said.

"You know," said Tommy, "I'm sorry about it. He's—well, he's a nice chap."

"They are, my dear fellow, they usually are. It isn't the skunks and the rats of a land who volunteer to go to the enemy's country. It's the brave men. We know that well enough. But there it is, the case is proved."

"No doubt whatever, you say?"

"No doubt at all. Among his chemical formulae was a list of people in the factory to be approached, as possible Fascist sympathizers. There was also a very clever scheme of sabotage and a chemical process that, applied to fertilizers, would have devastated large areas of food stocks. All well up Master Carl's street."

Rather unwillingly, Tommy said, secretly anathematizing Tuppence who had made him promise to say it:

"I suppose it's not possible that these things could have been planted on him?"

Mr. Grant smiled, rather a diabolical smile.

"Oh," he said. "Your wife's idea, no doubt."

"Well—er—yes, as a matter of fact it is."

"He's an attractive lad," said Mr. Grant tolerantly.

Then he went on:

"No, seriously, I don't think we can take that suggestion into account. He'd got a supply of secret ink, you know. That's a pretty good clinching test. And it wasn't obvious as it would have been if planted. It wasn't 'the mixture to be taken when required' on the washstand or anything like that. In fact, it was damned ingenious. Only come across the method once before and then it was waistcoat buttons. Steeped in the stuff, you know. When the fellow wants to use it, he soaks a button in water. Carl von Deinim's wasn't buttons. It was a shoe-lace. Pretty neat."

"Oh!" Something stirred in Tommy's mind—vague—wholly nebulous. . . .

Tuppence was quicker. As soon as he retailed the conversation to her, she seized on the salient point.

"A shoe-lace? Tommy, that explains it!"

"What?"

"Betty, you idiot! Don't you remember that funny thing she did in my room, taking out my laces and soaking them in water. I thought at the time it was a funny thing to think of doing. But, of course, she'd seen Carl do it and was imitating him. He couldn't risk her talking about it and so he arranged with that woman for her to be kidnapped."

Tommy said, "Then that's cleared up."

"Yes. It's nice when things begin to fall into shape. You can put them behind you and get on a bit."

"We need to get on."

Tuppence nodded.

The times were gloomy indeed. France had astonishingly and suddenly capitulated—to the bewilderment and dismay of her own people.

The destination of the French Navy was in doubt.

Now the coasts of France were entirely in the hands of Germany and the talk of invasion was no longer a remote contingency.

Tommy said:

"Carl von Deinim was only a link in the chain. Mrs. Perenna's the fountain head."

"Yes, we've got to get the goods on her. But it won't be easy."

"No. After all, if she's the brains of the whole thing, one can't expect it to be."

"Was M Mrs. Perenna?"

Tommy supposed she must be. He said slowly:

"You really think the girl isn't in this at all?"

"I'm quite sure of it."

Tommy sighed.

"Well, you should know. But if so, it's tough luck on her. First the man she loves—and then her mother. She's not going to have much left, is she?"

"We can't help that."

"Yes, but supposing we're wrong—that M or N is someone else?"

Tuppence said rather coldly:

"So you're still harping on that? Are you sure it isn't a case of wishful thinking?"

"What do you mean?"

"Sheila Perenna—that's what I mean."

"Aren't you being rather absurd, Tuppence?"

"No, I'm not. She's got round you, Tommy, just like any other man—"

Tommy replied angrily:

"Not at all. It's simply that I've got my own ideas."

"Which are?"

"I think I'll keep them to myself for a bit. We'll see which of us is right."

"Well, I think we've got to go all out after Mrs. Perenna. Find out where she goes, whom she meets—everything.

There must be a link somewhere. You'd better put Albert on to her this afternoon."

"You can do that. I'm busy."

"Why, what are you doing?"

Tommy said:

"I'm playing golf."

9

"Seems quite like old times, doesn't it, Madam?" said Albert. He beamed happily. Though now, in his middle years, running somewhat to fat, Albert had still the romantic boy's heart which had first led him into associations with Tommy and Tuppence in their young and adventurous days.

"Remember how you first came across me?" demanded Albert. "Cleanin' of the brasses, I was, in those top notch flats. Coo, wasn't that hall porter a nasty bit of goods? Always on to me, he was. And the day you come along and strung me a tale! Pack of lies it was, too, all about a crook called Ready Rita. Not but what some of it didn't turn out to be true. And since then, as you might say, I've never looked back. Many's the adventure we had afore we all settled down, so to speak."

Albert sighed, and by a natural association of ideas Tuppence inquired after the health of Mrs. Albert.

"Oh, the Missus is all right—but she doesn't take to the Welsh much, she says. Thinks they ought to learn proper English, and as for raids—why, they've had two there already, and holes in the field what you could put a motor car in, so she says. So—how's that for safety? Might as well be in Kensington, she says, where she wouldn't have to see all them melancholy trees and could get good clean milk in a bottle."

"I don't know," said Tuppence, suddenly stricken, "that we ought to get you into this, Albert."

"Nonsense, Madam," said Albert. "Didn't I try and join

up and they was so haughty they wouldn't look at me. Wait for my age group to be called up, they said. And me in the pink of health and only too eager to get at them perishing Germans—if you'll excuse the language. You just tell me how I can put a spoke in their wheel and spoil their goings on—and I'm there. Fifth Column, that's what we're up against, so the papers say—though what's happened to the other four they don't mention. But the long and short of it is, I'm ready to assist you and Captain Beresford in any way you like to indicate."

"Good. Now I'll tell you what we want you to do."

TWO

"How well do you know Bletchley?" asked Tommy, as he stepped off the tee and watched with approval his ball leaping down the centre of the fairway.

Commander Haydock who had also done a good drive had a pleased expression on his face as he shouldered his clubs and replied:

"Bletchley? Let me see. Oh! About nine months or so. He came here last Autumn."

"Friend of friends of yours, I think you said?" Tommy suggested mendaciously.

"Did I?" The Commander looked a little surprised. "No, I don't think so. Rather fancy I met him here at the Club."

"Bit of a mystery man, I gather?"

The Commander was clearly surprised this time.

"Mystery man? Old Bletchley?" He sounded frankly incredulous.

Tommy sighed inwardly. He supposed he was imagining things.

He played his next shot—and topped it. Haydock had a good iron shot that stopped just short of the green. As he rejoined the other, he said:

"What on earth makes you call Bletchley a mystery man? I should have said he was a painfully prosaic chap—typical Army. Bit set in his ideas and all that—narrow life, an Army life—but mystery!"

Tommy said vaguely:

"Oh, well, I just got the idea from something somebody said—"

They got down to the business of putting. The Commander won the hole.

"Three up and two to play," he remarked with satisfaction.

Then, as Tommy had hoped, his mind, free of the preoccupation of the match, harked back to what Tommy had said.

"What sort of mystery do you mean?" he asked.

Tommy shrugged his shoulders.

"Oh, it was just that nobody seemed to know much about him."

"He was in the Rugbyshires."

"Oh, you know that definitely?"

"Well, I—well, no, I don't know myself. I say, Meadowes, what's the idea? Nothing wrong about Bletchley, is there?"

"No, no, of course not." Tommy's disclaimer came hastily. He had started his hare. He could now sit back and watch the Commander's mind dodging after it.

"Always struck me as an almost absurdly typical sort of chap," said Haydock.

"Just so, just so."

"Ah, yes—see what you mean. Bit too much of a type, perhaps?"

"I'm leading the witness," thought Tommy. "Still perhaps something may crop up out of the old boy's mind."

"Yes, I do see what you mean," the Commander went on thoughtfully. "And now I come to think of it I've never actually come across anyone who knew Bletchley before he came down here. He doesn't have any old pals to stay— nothing of that kind."

"Ah!" said Tommy—and added, "Shall we play the bye? Might as well get a bit more exercise. It's a lovely evening."

They drove off, then separated to play their next shots. When they met again on the green, Haydock said abruptly:

"Tell me what you heard about him?"

"Nothing—nothing at all."

"No need to be so cautious with me, Meadowes. I hear all sorts of rumours. You understand? Everyone comes to me. I'm known to be pretty keen on the subject. What's the idea—that Bletchley isn't what he seems to be?"

"It was only the merest suggestion."

"What do they think he is? A Hun? Nonsense, the man's as English as you and I."

"Oh, yes, I'm sure he's quite all right."

"Why, he's always yelling for more foreigners to be interned. Look how violent he was against that young German chap—and quite right, too, it seems. I heard unofficially from the Chief Constable that they found enough to hang von Deinim a dozen times over. He'd got a scheme to poison the water supply of the whole country and he was actually working out a new gas—working on it in one of our factories. My God, the shortsightedness of our people! Fancy letting the fellow inside the place to begin with. Believe anything, our Government would! A young fellow has only to come to this country just before war starts and whine a bit about persecution and they shut both eyes and let him into all our secrets. They were just as dense about that fellow Hahn—"

Tommy had no intention of letting the Commander run ahead on the well-grooved track. He deliberately missed a putt.

"Hard lines," cried Haydock. He played a careful shot. The ball rolled into the hole.

"My hole. A bit off your game today. What were we talking about?"

Tommy said firmly:

"About Bletchley being perfectly all right."

"Of course. Of course. I wonder now—I did hear a rather funny story about him—didn't think anything of it at the time—"

Here, to Tommy's annoyance, they were hailed by two other men. The four returned to the clubhouse together and had drinks. After that, the Commander looked at his watch and remarked that he and Meadowes must be getting along. Tommy had accepted an invitation to supper with the Commander.

Smugglers' Rest was in its usual condition of apple pie order. A tall middle-aged manservant waited on them with the professional deftness of a waiter. Such perfect service was somewhat unusual to find outside of a London restaurant.

When the man had left the room, Tommy commented on the fact.

"Yes, I was lucky to get Appledore."

"How did you get hold of him?"

"He answered an advertisement as a matter of fact. He had excellent references, was clearly far superior to any of the others who applied and asked remarkably low wages. I engaged him on the spot."

Tommy said with a laugh:

"The war has certainly robbed us of most of our good restaurant service. Practically all good waiters were foreigners. It doesn't seem to come naturally to the Englishman."

"Bit too servile, that's why. Bowing and scraping doesn't come kindly to the English bulldog."

Sitting outside, sipping coffee, Tommy gently asked:

"What was it you were going to say on the links? Something about a funny story—apropos to Bletchley."

"What was it now? Hullo, did you see that? Light being shown out at sea. Where's my telescope!"

Tommy sighed. The stars in their courses seemed to be fighting against him. The Commander fussed into the house and out again, swept the horizon with his glass, outlined a whole system of signalling by the enemy to likely spots on shore, most of the evidence for which seemed to be nonexistent, and proceeded to give a gloomy picture of a successful invasion in the near future.

"No organization, no proper co-ordination. You're a L.D.V. yourself, Meadowes—you know what it's like. With a man like old Andrews in charge—"

This was well-worn ground. It was Commander Haydock's pet grievance. He ought to be the man in command and he was quite determined to oust Col. Andrews if it could possibly be done.

The manservant brought out whisky and liqueurs while the Commander was still holding forth.

"—and we're still honeycombed with spies—riddled with

'em. It was the same in the last war—hairdressers, waiters—"

Tommy, leaning back, catching the profile of Appledore as the latter hovered deft-footed, thought—"Waiters? You could call that fellow Fritz easier than Appledore. . . ."

Well, why not? The fellow spoke perfect English, true, but then many Germans did. They had perfected their English by years in English restaurants. And the racial type was not unlike. Fair-haired, blue-eyed—often betrayed by the shape of the head—yes, the head—where had he seen a head lately?

He spoke on an impulse. The words fitted in appropriately enough with what the Commander was just saying.

"All these damned forms to fill in. No good at all, Meadowes. Series of idiotic questions—"

Tommy said:

"I know. Such as—'What is your name? Answer N or M.' "

There was a swerve—a crash. Appledore, the perfect servant, had blundered. A stream of crème de menthe soaked over Tommy's cuff and hand.

The man stammered, "Sorry, sir."

Haydock blazed out in fury.

"You damned clumsy fool! What the Hell do you think you're doing?"

His usually red face was quite purple with anger. Tommy thought: "Talk of an Army temper—Navy beats it hollow!" Haydock continued with a stream of abuse. Appledore was abject in apologies.

Tommy felt uncomfortable for the man, but suddenly, as though by magic, the Commander's wrath passed and he was his hearty self again.

"Come along and have a wash. Beastly stuff. It would be the crème de menthe."

Tommy followed him indoors and was soon in the sumptuous bathroom with the innumerable gadgets. He carefully washed off the sticky sweet stuff. The Commander talked from the bedroom next door. He sounded a little shamefaced.

"Afraid I let myself go a bit. Poor old Appledore—he

knows I let go a bit more than I mean always."

Tommy turned from the washbasin drying his hands.
He did not notice that a cake of soap had slipped onto the
floor. His foot stepped on it. The linoleum was highly
polished.

A moment later Tommy was doing a wild ballet dancer
step. He shot across the bathroom, arms outstretched. One
came up heavily against the right hand tap of the bath, the
other pushed heavily against the side of a small bathroom
cabinet. It was an extravagant gesture never likely to be
achieved except by some catastrophe such as had just
occurred.

His foot skidded heavily against the end panel of the bath.

The thing happened like a conjuring trick. The bath slid
out from the wall, turning on a concealed pivot. Tommy
found himself looking into a dim recess. He had no doubt
whatever as to what occupied that recess. It contained a
transmitting wireless apparatus.

The Commander's voice had ceased. He appeared suddenly in the doorway. And with a click, several things fell
into place in Tommy's brain.

Had he been blind up to now? That jovial florid face—
the face of a "hearty Englishman"—was only a mask. Why
had he not seen it all along for what it was—the face of a
bad-tempered, overbearing Prussian officer. Tommy was
helped, no doubt, by the incident that had just happened.
For it recalled to him another incident, a Prussian bully
turning on a subordinate and rating him with the Junker's
true insolence. So had Commander Haydock turned on his
subordinate that evening when the latter had been taken
unawares.

And it all fitted in—it fitted in like magic. The double
bluff. The enemy agent Hahn, sent first, preparing the place,
employing foreign workmen, drawing attention to himself
and proceeding finally to the next stage in the plan, his own
unmasking by the gallant British sailor Commander Haydock. And then how natural that the Englishman should
buy the place and tell the story to everyone, boring them
by constant repetition. And so M, securely settled in his

appointed place with sea communications and his secret wireless and his staff officers at Sans Souci close at hand, N is ready to carry out Germany's plan.

Tommy was unable to resist a flash of genuine admiration. The whole thing had been so perfectly planned. He himself had never suspected Haydock—he had accepted Haydock as the genuine article—only a completely unforeseen accident had given the show away.

All this passed through Tommy's mind in a few seconds. He knew, only too well, that he was, that he must necessarily be in deadly peril. If only he could act the part of the credulous thick-headed Englishman well enough.

He turned to Haydock with what he hoped was a natural sounding laugh.

"By jove, one never stops getting surprises at your place. Was this another of Hahn's little gadgets? You didn't show me this the other day."

Haydock was standing very still. There was a tensity about his big body as it stood there blocking the door.

"More than a match for me," Tommy thought. "And there's that confounded servant, too."

For an instant Haydock stood as though moulded in stone, then he relaxed. He said with a laugh:

"Damned funny, Meadowes. You went skating over the floor like a ballet dancer! Don't suppose a thing like that would happen once in a thousand times. Dry your hands and come along into the other room."

Tommy followed him out of the bathroom. He was alert and tense in every muscle. Somehow or other he must get safely away from this house with his knowledge. Could he succeed in fooling Haydock? The latter's tone sounded natural enough.

With an arm round Tommy's shoulders, a casual arm, perhaps (or perhaps not), Haydock shepherded him into the sitting room. Turning, he shut the door behind them.

"Look here, old boy, I've got something to say to you."

His voice was friendly, natural—just a shade embarrassed. He motioned to Tommy to sit down.

"It's a bit awkward," he said. "Upon my word, it's a bit

awkward! Nothing for it, though, but to take you into my confidence. Only you'll have to keep dark about it, Meadowes. You understand that?"

Tommy endeavoured to throw an expression of eager interest upon his face.

Haydock sat down and drew his chair confidentially close.

"You see, Meadowes, it's like this. Nobody's supposed to know it but I'm working on Intelligence. M.I.42 B.X.— that's my department. Ever heard of it?"

Tommy shook his head and intensified the eager expression.

"Well, it's pretty secret. Kind of inner ring, if you know what I mean. We transmit certain information from here— but it would be absolutely fatal if that fact got out, you understand?"

"Of course, of course," said Mr. Meadowes. "Most interesting! Naturally you can count on me not to say a word."

"Yes, that's absolutely vital. The whole thing is extremely confidential."

"I quite understand. Your work must be most thrilling. Really most thrilling. I should like so much to know more about it—but I suppose I mustn't ask that?"

"No, I'm afraid not. It's very secret, you see."

"Oh, yes, I see. I really do apologize—a most extraordinary accident—"

He thought to himself:

"Surely he can't be taken in? He can't imagine I'd fall for this stuff?"

It seemed incredible to him. Then he reflected that vanity had been the undoing of many men. Commander Haydock was a clever man, a big fellow—this miserable chap Meadowes was a stupid Britisher—the sort of man who would believe anything! If only Haydock continued to think that.

Tommy went on talking. He displayed keen interest and curiosity. He knew he mustn't ask questions but—he supposed Commander Haydock's work must be very dangerous? Had he ever been in Germany, working there?

Haydock replied genially enough. He was intensely the British sailor now—the Prussian officer had disappeared. But Tommy, watching him with a new vision, wondered how he could ever have been deceived. The shape of the head—the line of the jaw—nothing British about them.

Presently Mr. Meadowes rose. It was the supreme test. Would it go off all right?

"I really must be going now—getting quite late—feel terribly apologetic, but can assure you will not say a word to anybody."

("It's now or never. Will he let me go or not? I must be ready—a straight to his jaw would be best—")

Talking amiably and with pleasurable excitement, Mr. Meadowes edged towards the door.

He was in the hall . . . he had opened the front door . . .

Through a door on the right he caught a glimpse of Appledore setting the breakfast things ready on a tray for the morning. ("The damned fool was going to let him get away with it!")

The two men stood in the porch, chatting—fixing up another match for next Saturday.

Tommy thought grimly: "There'll be no next Saturday for you, my boy."

Voices came from the road outside. Two men returning from a tramp on the headland. They were men that both Tommy and the Commander knew slightly. Tommy hailed them. They stopped. Haydock and he exchanged a few words with them, all standing at the gate, then Tommy waved a genial farewell to his host and stepped off with the two men.

He had got away with it.

Haydock, damned fool, had been taken in!

He heard Haydock go back to his house, go in and shut the door. Tommy tramped cheerfully down the hill with his two new-found friends.

Weather looked likely to change.

Old Monroe was off his game again.

That fellow Ashby refused to join the L.D.V. Said it was no damned good. Pretty thick, that. Young Marsh, the assistant caddy master, was a conscientious objector. Didn't Meadowes think that matter ought to be put up to the committee? There had been a pretty bad raid on Southampton, the night before last—quite a lot of damage done.

What did Meadowes think about Spain? Were they turning nasty? Of course, ever since the French collapse—

Tommy could have shouted aloud. Such good casual normal talk. A stroke of providence that these two men had turned up just at that moment.

He said goodbye to them at the gate of Sans Souci and turned in.

He walked the drive whistling softly to himself.

He had just turned the dark corner by the rhododendrons when something heavy descended on his head. He crashed forward, pitching into blackness and oblivion.

10

"Did you say three spades, Mrs. Blenkensop?"

Yes, Mrs. Blenkensop had said three spades. Mrs. Sprot, returning breathless from the telephone, saying: "And they've changed the time of the A.R.P. exam. again, it's *too* bad," demanded to have the bidding again.

Miss Minton, as usual, delayed things by ceaseless reiterations.

"Was it two clubs I said? Are you sure? I rather thought, you know, that it might have been on no trump— Oh, yes, of course, I remember now. Mrs. Cayley said one heart, didn't she? I was going to say one no trump, although I hadn't quite got the count, but I do think one should play a plucky game—and then Mrs. Cayley said one heart and so I had to go two clubs. I always think it's so difficult when one has two short suits—"

Sometimes, Tuppence thought to herself, it would save time if Miss Minton just put her hand down on the table to show them all. She was quite incapable of not telling exactly what was in it.

"So now we've got it right," said Miss Minton triumphantly. "One heart, two clubs."

"Two spades," said Tuppence.

"I passed, didn't I?" said Mrs. Sprot.

They looked at Mrs. Cayley, who was leaning forward listening.

Miss Minton took up the tale.

"Then Mrs. Cayley said two hearts and I said three diamonds."

"And I said three spades," said Tuppence.

"Pass," said Mrs. Sprot.

Mrs. Cayley sat in silence. At last she seemed to become aware that everyone was looking at her.

"Oh, dear." She flushed. "I'm so sorry. I thought perhaps Mr. Cayley needed me. I hope he's all right out there on the terrace."

She looked from one to the other of them.

"Perhaps, if you don't mind, I'd better just go and *see*. I heard rather an odd noise. Perhaps he's dropped his book."

She fluttered out of the window. Tuppence gave an exasperated sigh.

"She ought to have a string tied to her wrist," she said. "Then he could pull it when he wanted her."

"Such a devoted wife," said Miss Minton. "It's very nice to see it, isn't it?"

"Is it?" said Tuppence, who was feeling far from good-tempered.

The three women sat in silence for a minute or two.

"Where's Sheila tonight?" asked Miss Minton.

"She went to the pictures," said Mrs. Sprot.

"Where's Mrs. Perenna?" asked Tuppence.

"She said she was going to do accounts in her room," said Miss Minton. "Poor dear. So tiring, doing accounts."

"She's not been doing accounts all the evening," said Mrs. Sprot, "because she came in just now when I was telephoning in the hall."

"I wonder where she'd been," said Miss Minton, whose life was taken up with such small wonderments. "Not to the pictures, they wouldn't be out yet."

"She hadn't got a hat on," said Mrs. Sprot. "Nor a coat. Her hair was all anyhow and I think she'd been running or something. Quite out of breath. She ran upstairs without a word and she glared—positively glared at me—and I'm sure *I* hadn't done anything."

Mrs. Cayley reappeared at the window.

"Fancy," she said. "Mr. Cayley has walked all round the garden by himself. He quite enjoyed it, he said. Such a mild night."

She sat down again.

"Let me see—Oh, do you think we could have the bidding over again?"

Tuppence suppressed a rebellious sigh. They had the bidding all over again and she was left to play three spades.

Mrs. Perenna came in just as they were cutting for the next deal.

"Did you enjoy your walk?" asked Miss Minton.

Mrs. Perenna stared at her. It was a fierce and unpleasant stare. She said:

"I've not been out."

"Oh—oh—I thought Mrs. Sprot said you'd come in just now."

Mrs. Perenna said:

"I just went outside to look at the weather."

Her tone was disagreeable. She threw a hostile glance at the meek Mrs. Sprot, who flushed and looked frightened.

"Just fancy," said Mrs. Cayley, contributing her item of news, "Mr. Cayley walked all round the garden."

Mrs. Perenna said sharply:

"Why did he do that?"

Mrs. Cayley said:

"It is such a mild night. He hasn't even put on his second muffler and he *still* doesn't want to come in. I do *hope* he won't get a chill."

Mrs. Perenna said:

"There are worse things than chills. A bomb might come any minute and blow us all to bits!"

"Oh, dear, I hope it won't."

"Do you? *I* rather wish it would."

Mrs. Perenna went out of the window. The four bridge players stared after her.

"She seems very *odd* tonight," said Mrs. Sprot.

Miss Minton leaned forward.

"You don't think, do you—" She looked from side to side. They all leaned nearer together. Miss Minton said in a sibilant whisper:

"You don't suspect, do you, that she *drinks*?"

"Oh, dear," said Mrs. Cayley, "I wonder now. That

would explain it. She really is so—so unaccountable sometimes. What do you think, Mrs. Blenkensop?"

"Oh, I don't *really* think so. I think she's worried about
something. Er—it's your call, Mrs. Sprot."

"Dear me, what shall I say?" asked Mrs. Sprot, survey-
ing her hand.

Nobody volunteered to tell her, though Miss Minton,
who had been gazing with unabashed interest into her hand
might have been in a position to advise.

"That isn't Betty, is it?" demanded Mrs. Sprot, her head
upraised.

"No, it isn't," said Tuppence firmly.

She felt that she might scream unless they could get on
with the game.

Mrs. Sprot looked at her hand vaguely, her mind still
apparently maternal. Then she said:

"Oh, one diamond, I *think*."

The call went round. Mrs. Cayley led.

"When in doubt lead a trump, they say," she twittered,
and laid down the nine of diamonds.

A deep genial voice said:

" 'Tis the curse of Scotland that you've played there!"

Mrs. O'Rourke stood in the window. She was breathing
deeply—her eyes were sparkling. She looked sly and malicious. She advanced into the room.

"Just a nice quiet game of bridge, is it?"

"What's that in your hand?" asked Mrs. Sprot, with
interest.

" 'Tis a hammer," said Mrs. O'Rourke amiably. "I found
it lying in the drive. No doubt someone left it there."

"It's a funny place to leave a hammer," said Mrs. Sprot
doubtfully.

"It is that," agreed Mrs. O'Rourke.

She seemed in a particularly good humour. Swinging the
hammer by its handle she went out into the hall.

"Let me see," said Miss Minton. "What's trumps?"

The game proceeded for five minutes without further in-
terruption, and then Major Bletchley came in. He had been
to the pictures and proceeded to tell them in detail the plot
of *Wandering Minstrel*, laid in the reign of Richard the

First. The Major, as a military man, criticized at some length the Crusading battle scenes.

The rubber was not finished, for Mrs. Cayley, looking at her watch, discovered the lateness of the hour with shrill little cries of horror and rushed out to Mr. Cayley. The latter, as a neglected invalid, enjoying himself a great deal, coughing in a sepulchral manner, shivering dramatically and saying several times:

"*Quite* all right, my dear. I hope you enjoyed your game. It doesn't matter about *me* at all. Even if I *have* caught a severe chill, what does it really matter? There's a war on!"

TWO

At breakfast the next morning, Tuppence was aware at once of a certain tension in the atmosphere.

Mrs. Perenna, her lips pursed very tightly together, was distinctly acrid in the few remarks she made. She left the room with what could only be described as a flounce.

Major Bletchley, spreading marmalade thickly on his toast, gave vent to a deep chuckle.

"Touch of frost in the air," he remarked. "Well, well! Only to be expected, I suppose."

"Why, what has happened?" demanded Miss Minton, leaning forward eagerly, her thin neck twitching with pleasurable anticipation.

"Don't know that I ought to tell tales out of school," replied the Major irritatingly.

"Oh! Major Bletchley!"

"*Do* tell us," said Tuppence.

Major Bletchley looked thoughtfully at his audience: Miss Minton, Mrs. Blenkensop, Mrs. Cayley and Mrs. O'Rourke. Mrs. Sprot and Betty had just left. He decided to talk.

"It's Meadowes," he said. "Been out on the tiles all night. Hasn't come home yet."

"*What?*" exclaimed Tuppence.

Major Bletchley threw her a pleased and malicious glance. He enjoyed the discomfiture of the designing widow.

"Bit of a gay dog, Meadowes," he chortled. "The Perenna's annoyed. Naturally."

"Oh, dear," said Miss Minton, flushing painfully. Mrs. Cayley looked shocked. Mrs. O'Rourke merely chuckled.

"Mrs. Perenna told me already," she said. "Ah, well, the boys will be boys."

Miss Minton said eagerly:

"Oh, but surely—perhaps Mr. Meadowes has met with an accident. In the blackout, you know."

"Good old blackout," said Major Bletchley. "Responsible for a lot. I can tell you, it's been an eye-opener being on patrol in the L.D.V. Stopping cars and all that. The amount of wives just 'seeing their husbands home.' And different names on their identity cards! And the wife or the husband coming back the other way alone a few hours later. Ha ha!" He chuckled, then quickly composed his face as he received the full blast of Mrs. Blenkensop's disapproving stare.

"Human nature—a bit humorous, eh?" he said appeasingly.

"Oh, but Mr. Meadowes," bleated Miss Minton. "He may really have met with an accident. Been knocked down by a car."

"That'll be his story, I expect," said the Major. "Car hit him and knocked him out and he came to in the morning."

"He may have been taken to hospital."

"They'd have let us know. After all, he's carrying his identity card, isn't he?"

"Oh, dear," said Mrs. Cayley. "I wonder what Mr. Cayley will say?"

This rhetorical question remained unanswered. Tuppence, rising with an assumption of affronted dignity, got up and left the room.

Major Bletchley chuckled when the door closed behind her.

"Poor old Meadowes," he said. "The fair widow's annoyed about it. Thought she'd got her hooks into him."

"Oh, Major *Bletchley*," bleated Miss Minton.

Major Bletchley winked.

"Remember Sam in Dickens. *Beware of widders, Sammy*."

THREE

Tuppence was a little upset by Tommy's unannounced absence, but she tried to reassure herself. He might possibly have struck some hot trail and gone off upon it. The difficulties of communication with each other under such circumstances had been foreseen by them both, and they had agreed that the other one was not to be unduly perturbed by unexplained absences. They had arranged certain contrivances between them for such emergencies.

Mrs. Perenna had, according to Mrs. Sprot, been out last night. The vehemence of her own denial of the fact only made that absence of hers more interesting to speculate upon.

It was possible that Tommy had trailed her on her secret errand and had found something worth following up.

Doubtless he would communicate with Tuppence in his special way, or else turn up, very shortly.

Nevertheless, Tuppence was unable to avoid a certain feeling of uneasiness. She decided that in her rôle of Mrs. Blenkensop it would be perfectly natural to display some curiosity and even anxiety. She went without more ado in search of Mrs. Perenna.

Mrs. Perenna was inclined to be short with her upon the subject. She made it clear that such conduct on the part of one of her lodgers was not to be condoned or glossed over.

Tuppence exclaimed breathlessly:

"Oh, but he may have met with an *accident*. I'm sure he *must* have done. He's not at all that sort of man—not at all loose in his ideas, or *anything* of that kind. He must have been run down by a car or something."

"We shall probably soon hear one way or another," said Mrs. Perenna.

But the day wore on and there was no sign of Mr. Meadowes.

In the evening, Mrs. Perenna, urged on by the pleas of her boarders, agreed extremely reluctantly to ring up the police.

A sergeant called at the house with a notebook and took

particulars. Certain facts were then elicited. Mr. Meadowes
had left Commander Haydock's house at half past ten. From
there he had walked with a Mr. Walters and a Dr. Curtis as
far as the gate of Sans Souci, where he had said goodbye to
them and turned into the drive.

From that moment, Mr. Meadowes seemed to have disappeared into space.

In Tuppence's mind, two possibilities emerged from this.

When walking up the drive, Tommy may have seen Mrs.
Perenna coming towards him, have slipped into the bushes
and then have followed her. Having observed her rendezvous with some unknown person, he might then have followed the latter, whilst Mrs. Perenna returned to Sans Souci.
In that case, he was probably very much alive, and busy on
a trail. In which case the well-meant endeavours of the
police to find him might prove most embarrassing.

The other possibility was not so pleasant. It resolved itself into two pictures—one that of Mrs. Perenna returning
"out of breath and dishevelled"—the other, one that would
not be laid aside, a picture of Mrs. O'Rourke standing smiling in the window, holding a heavy hammer.

That hammer had horrible possibilities.

For what should a hammer be doing lying outside?

As to who had wielded it, that was most difficult. A good
deal depended on the exact time Mrs. Perenna had re-
entered the house. It was certainly somewhere in the neighbourhood of half past ten, but none of the bridge party
happened to have noted the time exactly. Mrs. Perenna had
declared vehemently that she had not been out except just
to look at the weather. But one does not get out of breath
just looking at the weather. It was clearly extremely vexing
to her to have been seen by Mrs. Sprot. With ordinary luck
the four ladies might have been safely accounted for as busy
playing bridge.

What had the time been exactly?

Tuppence found everybody extremely vague on the subject.

If the time agreed, Mrs. Perenna was clearly the most
likely suspect. But there were other possibilities. Of the
inhabitants of Sans Souci, three had been out at the time of

Tommy's return. Major Bletchley had been out at the cinema—but he had been to it alone, and the way that he had insisted on retailing the whole picture so meticulously might suggest to a suspicious mind that he was deliberately establishing an *alibi*.

Then there was the valetudinarian Mr. Cayley who had gone for a walk all round the garden. But for the accident of Mrs. Cayley's anxiety over her spouse, no one might have ever heard of that walk and might have imagined Mr. Cayley to have remained securely encased in rugs like a mummy in his chair on the terrace. (Rather unlike him, really, to risk the contamination of the night air so long.)

And there was Mrs. O'Rourke herself, swinging the hammer, and smiling . . .

FOUR

"What's the matter, Deb? You're looking worried, my sweet."

Deborah Beresford started and then laughed, looking frankly into Tony Marsdon's sympathetic brown eyes. She liked Tony. He had brains—was one of the most brilliant beginners in the coding department—and was thought likely to go far.

Deborah enjoyed her job, though she found it made somewhat strenuous demands on her powers of concentration. It was tiring, but it was worth while and it gave her a pleasant feeling of importance. This was real work—not just hanging about a hospital waiting for a chance to nurse.

She said:

"Oh, nothing. Just *family! You* know."

"Families *are* a bit trying. What's yours been up to?"

"It's my mother. To tell the truth I'm just a bit worried about her."

"Why? What's happened?"

"Well, you see, she went down to Cornwall to a frightfully trying old aunt of mine. Seventy-eight and completely ga ga."

"Sounds grim," commented the young man sympathetically.

"Yes, it was really very noble of mother. But she was rather hipped anyway because nobody seemed to want her in this war. Of course, she nursed and did things in the last one—but it's all quite different now, and they don't want these middle-aged people. They want people who are young and on the spot. Well, as I say, mother got a bit hipped over it all, and so she went off down to Cornwall to stay with Aunt Gracie, and she's been doing a bit in the garden, extra vegetable growing and all that."

"Quite sound," commented Tony.

"Yes, much the best thing she could do. She's quite active still, you know," said Deborah kindly.

"Well, that sounds all right."

"Oh, yes, it isn't *that*. I was quite happy about her—had a letter only two days ago sounding quite cheerful.

"What's the trouble, then?"

"The trouble is that I told Charles, who was going down to see his people in that part of the world, to go and look her up. And he did. And she wasn't there."

"Wasn't *there*?"

"No. And she hadn't been there! Not at all apparently!"

Tony looked a little embarrassed.

"Rather odd," he murmured. "Where's—I mean—your father?"

"Carrot Top? Oh, he's in Scotland somewhere. In one of those dreadful Ministries where they file papers in triplicate all day long."

"Your mother hasn't gone to join him perhaps?"

"She can't. He's in one of those area things where wives can't go."

"Oh—er—well, I suppose she's just sloped off somewhere."

Tony was decidedly embarrassed now—especially with Deborah's large worried eyes fixed plaintively upon him.

"Yes, but why? It's so *queer*. All her letters—talking about Aunt Gracie and the garden and everything."

"I know, I know," said Tony hastily. "Of course, she'd want you to think—I mean—nowadays—well, people *do* slope off now and again, if you know what I mean—"

Deborah's gaze, from being plaintive, became suddenly wrathful.

"If you think mother's just gone off week-ending with someone you're absolutely wrong. Absolutely. Mother and father are devoted to each other—really devoted. It's quite a joke in the family. She'd never—"

Tony said hastily:

"Of course not. Sorry. I really didn't mean—"

Deborah, her wrath appeased, creased her forehead.

"The odd thing is that someone the other day said they'd seen mother in Leahampton, of all places, and of course I said it couldn't be her because she was in Cornwall, but now I wonder—"

Tony, his match held to a cigarette, paused suddenly and the match went out.

"Leahampton?" he said sharply.

"Yes. Just the last place you could imagine mother going off to. Nothing to do and all old Colonels and maiden ladies."

"Doesn't sound a likely spot, certainly," said Tony.

He lit his cigarette and asked casually:

"What did your mother do in the last war?"

Deborah answered mechanically:

"Oh, nursed a bit and drove a General—army I mean, not a bus. All the usual sort of things."

"Oh, I thought perhaps she'd been like you—in the Intelligence."

"Oh, mother would never have had the head for this sort of work. I believe, though, that after the war she and father did do something in the sleuthing line. Secret papers and master spies—that sort of thing. Of course, the darlings exaggerate it all a good deal and make it all sound as though it had been frightfully important. We don't really encourage them to talk about it much because you know what one's family is—the same old story over and over again."

"Oh, rather," said Tony Marsdon heartily. "I quite agree."

It was on the following day that Deborah, returning to her lodging house, was puzzled by something unfamiliar in the appearance of her room.

It took her a few minutes to fathom what it was. Then she
rang the bell and demanded angrily of her landlady what
had happened to the big photograph that always stood on
the top of the chest of drawers.

Mrs. Rowley was aggrieved and resentful.

She couldn't say, she was sure. She hadn't touched it herself. Maybe Gladys—

But Gladys also denied having removed it. The man had
been there about the gas, she said hopefully.

But Deborah declined to believe that an employé of the
Gas Company would have taken a fancy to and removed the
portrait of a middle-aged lady.

Far more likely, in Deborah's opinion, that Gladys had
smashed the photograph frame and had hastily removed all
traces of the crime to the dustbin.

Deborah didn't make a fuss about it. Sometime or other
she'd get her mother to send her another photo.

She thought to herself with rising vexation:

"What's the old darling up to? She might tell me. Of
course, it's absolute nonsense to suggest, as Tony did, that
she's gone off with someone, but all the same it's very queer
. . ."

11

It was Tuppence's turn to talk to the fisherman on the end of the pier.

She had hoped against hope that Mr. Grant might have some comfort for her. But her hopes were soon dashed.

He stated definitely that no news of any kind had come from Tommy.

Tuppence said, trying her best to make her voice assured and business-like:

"There's no reason to suppose that anything has—happened to him?"

"None whatever. But let's suppose it has."

"What?"

"I'm saying—supposing it has. What about you?"

"Oh, I see—I—carry on, of course."

"That's the stuff. *There is time to weep after the battle.* We're in the thick of the battle now. And time is short. One piece of information you brought us has been proved correct. You overheard a reference to the *fourth*. The fourth referred to is the fourth of next month. It's the date fixed for the big attack on this country."

"You're sure?"

"Fairly sure. They're methodical people, our enemies. All their plans neatly made and worked out. Wish we could say the same of ourselves. Planning isn't our strong point. Yes, the Fourth is The Day. All these raids aren't the real thing—they're mostly reconnaissance—testing our defences and our reflexes to air attack. On the fourth comes the real thing."

"But if you know that—"

"We know The Day is fixed. We know, or think we know, roughly, *where* . . . (But we may be wrong there.) We're as ready as we can be. But it's the old story of the siege of Troy. They knew, as we know, all about the forces without. It's the forces within we want to know about. The men in the Wooden Horse! For they are the men who can deliver up the keys of the fortress. A dozen men in high places, in command in vital spots, by issuing conflicting orders, can throw the country into just that state of confusion necessary for the German plan to succeed. We've *got* to have inside information in time."

Tuppence said despairingly:

"I feel so futile—so inexperienced."

"Oh, you needn't worry about that. We've got experienced people working, all the experience and talent we've got— but when there's treachery within we can't tell who to trust. You and Beresford are the irregular forces. Nobody knows about you. That's why you've got a chance to succeed— that's why you *have* succeeded up to a certain point."

"Can't you put some of your people on to Mrs. Perenna? There *must* be some of them you can trust absolutely?"

"Oh, we've done that. Working from 'information received that Mrs. Perenna is a member of the I.R.A. with anti-British sympathies.' That's true enough, by the way— but we can't get proof of anything further. Not of the vital facts we want. So stick to it, Mrs. Beresford. Go on, and do your darnedest."

"The fourth," said Tuppence. "That's barely a week ahead?"

"It's a week exactly."

Tuppence clenched her hands.

"We *must* get *something!* I say *we* because I believe Tommy is on to something, and that that's why he hasn't come back. He's following up a lead. If I could only get something, too. I wonder now. If I—"

She frowned, planning a new form of attack.

TWO

"You see, Albert, it's a possibility."

"I see what you mean, Madam, of course. But I don't like the idea very much, I must say."

"I think it might work."

"Yes, Madam, but it's exposing yourself to attack—that's what I don't like—and I'm sure the master wouldn't like it."

"We've tried all the usual ways. That is to say, we've done what we could keeping under cover. It seems to me that now the only chance is to come out into the open."

"You are aware, Madam, that thereby you may be sacrificing an advantage?"

"You're frightfully B.B.C. in your language this afternoon, Albert," said Tuppence, with some exasperation.

Albert looked slightly taken aback and reverted to a more natural form of speech.

"I was listening to a very interesting talk on pond life last night," he explained.

"We've no time to think about pond life now," said Tuppence.

"Where's Captain Beresford, that's what I'd like to know?"

"So should I," said Tuppence, with a pang.

"Don't seem natural, his disappearing without a word. He ought to have tipped you the wink by now. That's why—"

"Yes, Albert?"

"What I mean is, if *he's* come out in the open, perhaps *you'd* better not."

He paused to arrange his ideas and then went on.

"I mean, they've blown the gaff on *him*, but *they mayn't know about you*—and so it's up to you to keep under cover still."

"I wish I could make up my mind," sighed Tuppence.

"Which way were you thinking of managing it, Madam?"

Tuppence murmured thoughtfully:

"I thought I might lose a letter I'd written—make a lot of fuss about it, seem very upset. Then it would be found in the hall and Beatrice would probably put it on the hall table. Then the right person would get a look at it."

"What would be in the letter?"

"Oh, roughly—that I'd been successful in discovering the identity of the person in question and that I was to make a full report personally tomorrow. Then, you see, Albert, N or M would have to come out in the open and have a shot at eliminating me."

"Yes, and maybe they'd manage it, too."

"Not if I was on my guard. They'd have, I think, to decoy me away somewhere—some lonely spot. That's where you'd come in—because they don't know about you."

"I'd follow them up and catch them red-handed, so to speak?"

Tuppence nodded.

"That's the idea. I must think it out carefully—I'll meet you tomorrow."

THREE

Tuppence was just emerging from the local lending library with what had been recommended to her as a "nice book" clasped under her arm when she was startled by a voice saying:

"Mrs. Beresford."

She turned abruptly to see a tall, dark young man with an agreeable but slightly embarrassed smile.

He said:

"Er—I'm afraid you don't remember me?"

Tuppence was thoroughly used to the formula. She could have predicted with accuracy the words that were coming next.

"I—er—came to the flat with Deborah one day."

Deborah's friends! So many of them, and all, to Tuppence, looking singularly alike! Some dark like this young man, some fair, an occasional red-haired one—but all cast in the same mould—pleasant, well-mannered, their hair, in

Tuppence's view, just slightly too long. (But when this was hinted, Deborah would say, "Oh, *mother*, don't be so terribly 1916. I can't *stand* short hair.")

Annoying to have run across and been recognized by one of Deborah's young men just now. However, she could probably soon shake him off.

"I'm Antony Marsdon," explained the young man.

Tuppence murmured mendaciously, "Oh, of course," and shook hands.

Tony Marsdon went on:

"I'm awfully glad to have found you, Mrs. Beresford. You see, I'm working at the same job as Deborah, and as a matter of fact something rather awkward has happened."

"Yes?" said Tuppence. "What is it?"

"Well, you see, Deborah's found out that you're not down in Cornwall as she thought, and that makes it a bit awkward, doesn't it, for you?"

"Oh, bother," said Tuppence, concerned. "How did she find out?"

Tony Marsdon explained. He went on rather diffidently:

"Deborah, of course, has no idea of what you're really doing."

He paused discreetly, and then went on:

"It's important, I imagine, that she shouldn't know. My job, actually, is rather the same line. I'm supposed to be just a beginner in the Coding Department. Really my instructions are to express views that are mildly Fascist— admiration of the German system, insinuations that a working alliance with Hitler wouldn't be a bad thing—all that sort of thing—just to see what response I get. There's a good deal of rot going on, you see, and we want to find out who's at the bottom of it."

"Not everywhere," thought Tuppence.

"But as soon as Deb told me about you," continued the young man, "I thought I'd better come straight down and warn you so that you could cook up a likely story. You see, I happen to know what you are doing and that it's of vital importance. It would be fatal if any hint of who you are got about. I thought perhaps you could make it seem as though you'd joined Captain Beresford in Scotland or wherever he is. You might say that you'd been allowed to work with him there."

"I might do that, certainly," said Tuppence thoughtfully.

Tony Marsdon said anxiously:

"You don't think I'm butting in?"

"No, no, I'm very grateful to you."

Tony said rather inconsequentially:

"I'm—well—you see—I'm rather fond of Deborah."

Tuppence flashed him an amused quick glance.

How far away it seemed, that world of attentive young men and Deb with her rudeness to them that never seemed to put them off. This young man was, she thought, quite an attractive specimen.

She put aside what she called to herself "peace time thoughts" and concentrated on the present situation.

After a moment or two she said slowly:

"My husband isn't in Scotland."

"Isn't he?"

"No, he's down here with me. At least he was! Now—he's disappeared."

"I say, that's bad—or isn't it? Was he on to something?"

Tuppence nodded.

"I think so. That's why I don't think that his disappearing like this is really a bad sign. I think, sooner or later, he'll communicate with me—in his own way." She smiled a little.

Tony said, with some slight embarrassment:

"Of course, you know the game well, I expect. But you ought to be careful."

Tuppence nodded.

"I know what you mean. Beautiful heroines in books are always easily decoyed away. But Tommy and I have our methods. We've got a slogan." She smiled. *"Penny plain and tuppence coloured."*

"What?" The young man stared at her as though she had gone mad.

"I ought to explain that my family nickname is Tuppence."

"Oh, I see." The young man's brow cleared. "Ingenious —what?"

"I hope so."

"I don't want to butt in—but couldn't I help in any way?"

"Yes," said Tuppence thoughtfully, "I think perhaps you might."

12

After long aeons of unconsciousness, Tommy began to be aware of a fiery ball swimming in space. In the centre of the fiery ball was a core of pain, the universe shrank, the fiery ball swung more slowly—he discovered suddenly that the nucleus of it was his own aching head.

Slowly he became aware of other things—of cold cramped limbs, of hunger, of an inability to move his lips.

Slower and slower swung the fiery ball . . . It was now Thomas Beresford's head and it was resting on solid ground. Very solid ground. In fact on something suspiciously like stone.

Yes, he was lying on hard stones, and he was in pain, unable to move, extremely hungry, cold and uncomfortable.

Surely, although Mrs. Perenna's beds had never been unduly soft, this could not be—

Of course—Haydock! The wireless! The German waiter! Turning in at the gates of Sans Souci . . .

Someone, creeping up behind him, had struck him down. That was the reason of his aching head.

And he'd thought he'd got away with it all right! So Haydock, after all, hadn't been quite such a fool?

Haydock? Haydock had gone back into Smugglers' Rest and closed the door. How had he managed to get down the hill and be waiting for Tommy in the grounds of Sans Souci?

It couldn't be done. Not without Tommy seeing him.

The manservant, then? Had he been sent ahead to lie in wait? But surely, as Tommy had crossed the hall, he had

seen Appledore in the kitchen of which the door was slightly
ajar. Or did he only fancy he had seen him? Perhaps that
was the explanation.

Anyway it didn't matter. The thing to do was to find out
where he was now.

His eyes, becoming accustomed to the darkness, picked
out a small rectangle of dim light. A window or small
grating. The air smelled chill and musty. He was, he fancied,
lying in a cellar. His hands and feet were tied and a gag in
his mouth was secured by a bandage.

"Seems rather as though I'm for it," thought Tommy.

He tried gingerly to move his limbs or body, but he
could not succeed.

At that moment, there was a faint creaking sound and a
door somewhere behind him was pushed open. A man with
a candle came in. He set down the candle on the floor.
Tommy recognized Appledore. The latter disappeared again
and then returned carrying a tray on which were a jug of
water, a glass and some bread and cheese.

Stooping down he first tested the cords binding the other's
limbs. He then touched the gag.

He said in a quiet level voice:

"I am about to take this off. You will then be able to eat
and drink. If, however, you make the slightest sound, I
shall replace it immediately."

Tommy tried to nod his head, which proved impossible,
so he opened and shut his eyes several times instead.

Appledore, taking this for consent, carefully unknotted
the bandage.

His mouth freed, Tommy spent some few minutes easing
his jaw. Appledore held the glass of water to his lips. He
swallowed at first with difficulty, then more easily. The
water did him a world of good.

He murmured stiffly:

"That's better. I'm not quite so young as I was. Now for
the eats, Fritz—or is it Franz?"

The man said quietly:

"My name here is Appledore."

He held the slice of bread and cheese up and Tommy bit
at it hungrily.

The meal washed down with some more water, he then asked:

"And what's the next part of the programme?"

For answer, Appledore picked up the gag again.

Tommy said quickly:

"I want to see Commander Haydock."

Appledore shook his head. Deftly he replaced the gag and went out.

Tommy was left to meditate in darkness. He was awakened from a confused sleep by the sound of the door reopening. This time Haydock and Appledore came in together. The gag was removed and the cords that held his arms were loosened so that he could sit up and stretch his arms.

Haydock had an automatic pistol with him.

Tommy, without much inward confidence, began to play his part.

He said indignantly:

"Look here, Haydock, what's the meaning of all this? I've been set upon—kidnapped—"

The Commander was gently shaking his head.

He said:

"Don't waste your breath. It's not worth it."

"Just because you're a member of our Secret Service, you think you can—"

Again the other shook his head.

"No, no, Meadowes. You weren't taken in by that story. No need to keep up the pretense."

But Tommy showed no signs of discomfiture. He argued to himself that the other could not really be sure. If he continued to play his part—

"Who the devil do you think you are?" he demanded. "However great your powers you've no right to behave like this. I'm prefectly capable of holding my tongue about any of our vital secrets!"

The other said coldly:

"You do your stuff very well, but I may tell you that it's immaterial to me whether you're a member of the British Intelligence, or merely a muddling amateur—"

"Of all the damned cheek—"

"Cut it out, Meadowes."

"I tell you—"

Haydock thrust a ferocious face forwards.

"Be quiet, damn you. Earlier on it would have mattered to find out who you were and who sent you. Now it doesn't matter. The time's short, you see. And you didn't have the chance to report to anyone what you'd found out."

"The police will be looking for me as soon as I'm reported missing."

Haydock showed his teeth in a sudden gleam.

"I've had the police here this evening. Good fellows— both friends of mine. They asked me all about Mr. Meadowes. Very concerned about his disappearance. How he seemed that evening—what he said. They never dreamed, how should they, that the man they were talking about was practically underneath their feet where they were sitting. It's quite clear, you see, that you left this house well and alive. They'd never dream of looking for you here."

"You can't keep me here forever," Tommy said vehemently.

Haydock said with a resumption of his most British manner:

"It won't be necessary, my dear fellow. Only until to-morrow night. There's a boat due in at my little cove—and we're thinking of sending you on a voyage for your health —though actually I don't think you'll be alive, or even on board, when they arrive at their destination."

"I wonder you didn't knock me on the head straight away."

"It's such hot weather, my dear fellow. Just occasionally our sea communications are interrupted, and if that were to be so—well, a dead body on the premises has a way of announcing its presence."

"I see," said Tommy.

He did see. The issue was perfectly clear. He was to be kept alive until the boat arrived. Then he would be killed— or drugged—and taken out to sea. Nothing would ever connect his body, when found, with Smugglers' Rest.

"I just came along," continued Haydock, speaking in the most natural manner, "to ask whether there is anything we could—er—do for you—afterwards?"

Tommy reflected. Then he said:

"Thanks—but I won't ask you to take a lock of my hair to the little woman in St. John's Wood, or anything of that kind. She'll miss me when pay day comes along—but I daresay she'll find a friend elsewhere."

At all costs, he felt, he must create the impression that he was playing a lone hand. So long as no suspicion attached itself to Tuppence then the game might still be won through, though he was not there to play it.

"As you please," said Haydock. "If you did care to send a message to—your friend—we would see that it was delivered."

So he was, after all, anxious to get a little information about this unknown Mr. Meadowes? Very well, then, Tommy would keep him guessing.

He shook his head.

"Nothing doing," he said.

"Very well." With an appearance of the utmost indifference Haydock nodded to Appledore. The latter replaced the bonds and the gag. The two men went out, locking the door behind them.

Left to his reflections, Tommy felt anything but cheerful. Not only was he faced with the prospect of rapidly approaching death but he had no means of leaving any clue behind him as to the information he had discovered.

His body was completely helpless. His brain felt singularly inactive. Could he, he wondered, have utilized Haydock's suggestion of a message? Perhaps if his brain had been working better . . . But he could think of nothing helpful.

There was, of course, still Tuppence. But what could Tuppence do? As Haydock had just pointed out, Tommy's disappearance would not be connected with him. Tommy had left Smuggler's Rest alive and well. The evidence of two independent witnesses would confirm that. Whoever Tuppence might suspect, it would not be Haydock. And she might not suspect at all. She might think that he was merely following up a trail.

Damn it all, if only he had been more on his guard—

There was a little light in the cellar. It came through the grating which was high up in one corner. If only he could get his mouth free, could shout for help. Somebody might hear, though it was very unlikely.

For the next half hour he busied himself straining at the cords that bound him and trying to bite through the gag. It was all in vain, however. The people who had adjusted those things knew their business.

It was, he judged, late afternoon. Haydock, he fancied, had gone out; he had heard no sounds from overhead.

Confound it all, he was probably playing golf, speculating at the clubhouse over what could have happened to Meadowes!

"Dined with me night before last—seemed quite normal then. Just vanished into the blue."

Tommy writhed with fury. That hearty English manner! Was everyone blind not to see that bullet-headed Prussian skull? He himself hadn't seen it. Wonderful what a first class actor could get away with.

So here he was—a failure—an ignominious failure—trussed up like a chicken, with no one to guess where he was.

If only Tuppence could have second sight! She might suspect. She had, sometimes, an uncanny insight . . .

What was that?

He strained his ears listening to a far-off sound.

Only some man humming a tune.

And here he was, unable to make a sound to attract anyone's attention.

The humming came nearer. A most untuneful noise.

But the tune, though mangled, was recognizable. It dated from the last war—had been revived for this one.

"If you were the only girl in the world and I was the only boy."

How often he had hummed that in 1917.

Dash this fellow. Why couldn't he sing in tune?

Suddenly Tommy's body grew taut and rigid. Those particular lapses were strangely familiar. Surely there was

only one person who always went wrong in that one particular place and in that one particular way!

"Albert, by Gosh!" thought Tommy.

Albert prowling round Smugglers' Rest. Albert quite
close at hand, and here was he, trussed up, unable to move
hand or foot, unable to make a sound . . .

Wait a minute. Was he?

There was just one sound—not so easy with the mouth
shut as with the mouth open, but it could be done.

Desperately Tommy began to snore. He kept his eyes
closed, ready to feign a deep sleep if Appledore should
come down, and he snored, he snored . . .

Short snore, short snore, short snore—pause—long snore,
long snore, long snore—pause—short snore, short snore,
short snore . . .

TWO

Albert, when Tuppence had left him, was deeply
perturbed.

With the advance of years he had become a person of
slow mental processes, but those processes were tenacious.

The state of affairs in general seemed to him quite wrong.

The War was all wrong to begin with

"Those Germans," thought Albert gloomily and almost
without rancour. Heiling Hitler and goose-stepping and
over-running the world and bombing and machine-gunning
and generally making pestilential nuisances of themselves.
They'd got to be stopped, no two ways about it—and so far
it seemed as though nobody had been able to stop them.

And now here was Mrs. Beresford, a nice lady if there
ever was one, getting herself mixed up in trouble and looking out for more trouble, and how was he going to stop her?
Didn't look as though he could. Up against this Fifth
Column and a nasty lot they must be. Some of 'em English
born, too! A disgrace, that was!

And the master who was always the one to hold the
missus back from her impetuous ways—the master was
missing.

Albert didn't like that at all. It looked to him as though

"those Germans" might be at the bottom of that.

Yes, it looked bad, it did. Looked as though he might have copped one.

Albert was not given to the exercise of deep reasoning. Like most Englishmen, he felt something strongly and proceeded to muddle around until he had, somehow or other, cleared up the mess. Deciding that the master had got to be found, Albert, rather after the manner of a faithful dog, set out to find him.

He acted upon no settled plan, but proceeded in exactly the same way as he was wont to embark upon the search for his wife's handbag or his own spectacles when either of those essential articles was mislaid. That is to say, he went to the place where he had last seen the missing objects and started from there.

In this case, the last thing known about Tommy was that he had dined with Commander Haydock at Smugglers' Rest and had then returned to Sans Souci and had been last seen turning in at the gate.

Albert, accordingly, climbed the hill as far as the gate of Sans Souci and spent some five minutes staring hopefully at the gate. Nothing of a scintillating character having occurred to him, he sighed and wandered slowly up the hill to Smugglers' Rest.

Albert, too, had visited the Ornate Cinema that week, and had been powerfully impressed by the theme of *Wandering Minstrel*. Romantic, it was! He could not but be struck by the similarity of his own predicament. He, like that hero of the screen, Gary Cooper, was a faithful Blondel seeking his imprisoned master. Like Blondel, he had fought at that master's side in bygone days. Now his master was betrayed by treachery, and there was none but his faitful Blondel to seek for him and restore him to the loving arms of Queen Berengaria.

Albert heaved a sigh as he remembered the melting strains of *Richard, O mon roi* which the faithful troubadour had crooned so feelingly beneath tower after tower.

Pity he himself wasn't better at picking up a tune. Took him a long time to get hold of a tune, it did. His lips shaped themselves into a tentative whistle. Begun playing the old tunes again lately, they had.

"If you were the only girl in the world and I was the only boy—"

Albert paused to survey the neat white painted gate of Smugglers' Rest. That was it, that was where the master had gone to dinner.

He went up the hill a little further and came out on the downs.

Nothing here. Nothing but grass and a few sheep.

The gate of Smugglers' Rest swung open and a car passed out. A big man in plus fours with golf clubs drove out and down the hill.

"That would be Commander Haydock, that would," Albert deduced.

He wandered down again and stared at Smugglers' Rest. A tidy little place. Nice bit of garden. Nice view.

He eyed it benignly.

"I would say such wonderful things to you," he hummed.

Through a side door of the house a man came out with a hoe and passed out of sight through a little gate.

Albert, who grew nasturtiums and a bit of lettuce in his back garden, was instantly interested.

He edged nearer to Smugglers' Rest and passed through the open gate. Yes, tidy little place.

He circled slowly round it. Some way below him, reached by steps, was a flat plateau planted as a vegetable garden. The man who had come out of the house was busy down there.

Albert watched him with interest for some minutes. Then he turned to contemplate the house.

Tidy little place, he thought for the third time. Just the sort of place a retired Naval gentleman would like to have. This was where the master had dined that night.

Slowly Albert circled round and round the house. He looked at it much as he had looked at the gate of Sans Souci —hopefully, as though asking it to tell him something.

And as he went he hummed softly to himself, a twentieth century Blondel in search of his master.

"There would be such wonderful things to do," hummed

Albert. *"I would say such wonderful things to you. There would be such wonderful things to do—"* Gone wrong somewhere, hadn't he? He'd hummed that bit before.

Hullo! Funny. So the Commander kept pigs, did he? A long drawn grunt came to him. Funny—seemed almost as though it were underground. Funny place to keep pigs.

Couldn't be pigs. No, it was someone having a bit of shut-eye. Bit of shut-eye in the cellar, so it seemed . . .

Right kind of day for a snooze, but funny place to go for it. Humming like a bumble bee, Albert approached nearer.

That's where it was coming from—through that little grating. Grunt, grunt, grunt. Snoooooore. Snoooooore. Snoooooore—grunt, grunt, grunt. Funny sort of snore—reminded him of something . . .

"Coo!" said Albert. "That's what it is—S.O.S.—Dot, dot, dot, dash, dash, dash, dot, dot, dot."

He looked round him with a quick glance.

Then, kneeling down, he tapped a soft message on the iron grille of the little window of the cellar.

13

Although Tuppence went to bed in an optimistic frame of mind, she suffered a severe reaction in those waking hours of early dawn when human *morale* sinks to its lowest.

On descending to breakfast, however, her spirits were raised by the sight of a letter on her plate addressed in a painfully backhanded script.

This was no communication from Douglas, Raymond or Cyril, or any other of the camouflaged correspondence that arrived punctually for her, and which included this morning a brightly coloured Bonzo postcard with a scrawled "Sorry I haven't written before. All well, Maudie" on it.

Tuppence thrust this aside and opened the letter.

DEAR PATRICIA [it ran],

Auntie Grace is, I am afraid, much worse today. The doctors do not actually say she is sinking, but I am afraid that there cannot be much hope. If you want to see her before the end I think it would be well to come today. If you will take the 10:20 train to Yarrow, a friend will meet you with his car.

Shall look forward to seeing you again, dear, in spite of the melancholy reason.

Yours ever,

PENELOPE PLAYNE.

It was all Tuppence could do to restrain her jubilation. Good old Penny Playne.

With some difficulty she assumed a mourning expression —and sighed heavily as she laid the letter down.

To the two sympathetic listeners present, Mrs. O'Rourke and Miss Minton, she imparted the contents of the letter, and enlarged freely on the personality of Aunt Gracie, her indomitable spirit, her indifference to air raids and danger, and her vanquishment by illness. Miss Minton tended to be curious as to the exact nature of Aunt Gracie's sufferings and compared them interestedly with the disease of her own cousin Selina. Tuppence, hovering slightly between dropsy and diabetes, found herself slightly confused, but compromised on complications with the kidneys. Mrs. O'Rourke displayed an avid interest as to whether Tuppence would benefit pecuniarily by the old lady's death and learned that dear Cyril had always been Aunt Gracie's favourite grandnephew as well as being her god-son.

After breakfast Tuppence rang up the tailor's and cancelled a fitting of a coat and skirt for that afternoon, and then sought out Mrs. Perenna and explained that she might be away from home for a night or two.

Mrs. Perenna expressed the usual conventional sentiments. She looked tired this morning, and had an anxious harassed expression.

"Still no news of Mr. Meadowes," she said. "It really is *most* odd, is it not?"

"I'm sure he must have met with an accident," sighed Mrs. Blenkensop. "I always said so."

"Oh, but surely, Mrs. Blenkensop, the accident would have been reported by this time."

"Well, what do you think?" asked Tuppence.

Mrs. Perenna shook her head.

"I really don't know *what* to say. I quite agree that he can't have gone away of his own free will. He would have sent word by now."

"It was always a most unjustified suggestion," said Mrs. Blenkensop warmly. "That horrid Major Bletchley started it. No, if it isn't an accident, it must be loss of memory. I believe that is far more common than is generally known, especially at times of stress like those we are living through now."

Mrs. Perenna nodded her head. She pursed up her lips with rather a doubtful expression. She shot a quick look at Tuppence.

"You know, Mrs. Blenkensop," she said, "we don't know very much *about* Mr. Meadowes, do we?"

Tuppence said sharply: "What do you mean?"

"Oh, please don't take me up so sharply. *I* don't believe it—not for a minute."

"Don't believe what?"

"This story that's going around."

"What story? I haven't heard anything."

"No—well—perhaps people wouldn't tell you. I don't really know how it started. I've an idea that Mr. Cayley mentioned it first. Of course he's rather a suspicious man, if you know what I mean?"

Tuppence contained herself with as much patience as possible.

"Please tell me," she said.

"Well, it was just a suggestion, you know, that Mr. Meadowes might be an enemy agent—one of these dreadful Fifth Column people."

Tuppence put all she could of an outraged Mrs. Blenkensop into her indignant:

"I never *heard* of such an absurd idea!"

"No. I don't think there's anything in it. But, of course, Mr. Meadowes *was* seen about a good deal with that German boy—and I believe he asked a lot of questions about the chemical processes at the factory—and so people think that perhaps the two of them might have been working together."

Tuppence said:

"*You* don't think there's any doubt about Carl, do you, Mrs. Perenna?"

She saw a quick spasm distort the other woman's face.

"I wish I *could* think it was not true."

Tuppence said gently:

"Poor Sheila . . ."

Mrs. Perenna's eyes flashed.

"Her heart's broken, the poor child. Why should it be

that way? Why couldn't it be someone else she set her heart upon?"

Tuppence shook her head.

"Things don't happen that way."

"You're right." The other spoke in a deep, bitter voice. "It's got to be the way things tear you to pieces . . . It's got to be sorrow and bitterness and dust and ashes. I'm sick of the cruelty—the unfairness of this world. I'd like to smash it and break it—and let us all start again near to the earth and without these rules and laws and the tyranny of nation over nation. I'd like—"

A cough interrupted her. A deep, throaty cough. Mrs. O'Rourke was standing in the doorway, her vast bulk filling the aperture completely.

"Am I interrupting now?" she demanded.

Like a sponge across a slate, all evidence of Mrs. Perenna's outburst vanished from her face—leaving in its wake only the mild worried face of the proprietress of a guest house whose guests were causing trouble.

"No, indeed, Mrs. O'Rourke," she said. "We were just talking about what had become of Mr. Meadowes. It's amazing the police can find no trace of him."

"Ah, the police!" said Mrs. O'Rourke in tones of easy contempt. "What good would they be? No good at all, at all! Only fit for finding motor cars, and dropping on poor wretches who haven't taken out their dog licenses."

"What's your theory, Mrs. O'Rourke?" asked Tuppence.

"You'll have been hearing the story that's going about?"

"About his being a Fascist, and an enemy agent—yes," said Tuppence coldly.

"It might be true now," said Mrs. O'Rourke thoughtfully, "for there's been something about the man that's intrigued me from the beginning. I've watched him, you know." She smiled directly at Tuppence—and like all Mrs. O'Rourke's smiles it had a vaguely terrifying quality—the smile of an ogress. "He'd not the look of a man who'd retired from business and had nothing to do with himself. If I was backing my judgment, I'd say he came here with a purpose."

"And when the police got on his track he disappeared, is that it?" demanded Tuppence.

"It might be so," said Mrs. O'Rourke. "What's your opinion, Mrs. Perenna?"

"I don't know," sighed Mrs. Perenna. "It's a most vexing thing to happen. It makes so much *talk.*"

"Ah! talk won't hurt you. They're happy now out there on the terrace wondering and surmising. They'll have it in the end that the quiet inoffensive man was going to blow us all up in our beds with bombs."

"You haven't told us what you think," said Tuppence.

Mrs. O'Rourke smiled, that same slow ferocious smile.

"I'm thinking that the man is safe somewhere—quite safe . . ."

Tuppence thought:

"She might say that if she knew . . . But he isn't where she thinks he is!"

She went up to her room to get ready. Betty Sprot came running out of the Cayleys' bedroom with a smile of mischievous and impish glee on her face.

"What have you been up to, minx?" demanded Tuppence.

Betty gurgled.

"Goosey, goosey gander . . ."

Tuppence chanted:

"Whither will you wander? *Up*stairs!" She snatched up Betty high over her head. *"Downstairs!"* She rolled her on the floor—

At this minute Mrs. Sprot appeared and Betty was led off to be attired for her walk.

"Hide?" said Betty hopefully. "Hide?"

"You can't play hide and seek now," said Mrs. Sprot.

Tuppence went into her room and donned her hat. (A nuisance having to wear a hat—Tuppence Beresford never did—but Patricia Blenkensop would certainly wear one, Tuppence felt.)

Somebody, she noted, had altered the position of the hats in her hat cupboard. Had someone been searching her room? Well, let them. They wouldn't find anything to cast doubt on blameless Mrs. Blenkensop.

She left Penelope Playne's letter artistically on the dressing table and went downstairs and out of the house.

It was ten o'clock as she turned out of the gate. Plenty of

time. She looked up at the sky and in doing so stepped into a dark puddle by the gatepost, but without apparently noticing it she went on.

Her heart was dancing wildly. Success—success—they were going to succeed.

TWO

Yarrow was a small country station where the village was some distance from the railway.

Outside the station a car was waiting. A good looking young man was driving it. He touched his peaked cap to Tuppence, but the gesture seemed hardly natural.

Tuppence kicked the off side tire dubiously.

"Isn't this rather flat?"

"We haven't far to go, Madam."

She nodded and got in.

They drove, not towards the village, but towards the downs. After winding up over a hill, they took a side track that dropped sharply into a deep cleft. From the shadow of a small copse of trees a figure stepped out to meet them. The car stopped and Tuppence, getting out, went to meet Antony Marsdon.

"Beresford's all right," he said quickly. "We located him yesterday. He's a prisoner—the other side got him—and for good reasons he's remaining put for another twelve hours. You see, there's a small boat due in at a certain spot—and we want to catch her badly. That's why Beresford's lying low—we don't want to give the show away until the last minute."

He looked at her anxiously.

"You do understand, don't you?"

"Oh, yes!" Tuppence was staring at a curious tangled mass of canvas material half hidden by the trees.

"He'll be absolutely all right," continued the young man earnestly.

"Of course Tommy will be all right," said Tuppence impatiently. "You needn't talk to me as though I were a child of two. We're both ready to run a few risks. What's that thing over there?"

"Well—" the young man hesitated. "That's just it. I've been ordered to put a certain proposition before you. But—but, well, frankly, I don't like doing it. You see—"

Tuppence treated him to a cold stare.

"Why don't you like doing it?"

"Well—dash it—you're Deborah's mother. And I mean —what would Deb say to me if—if—"

"If I got it in the neck?" inquired Tuppence. "Personally, if I were you, I shouldn't mention it to her. The man who said explanations were a mistake was quite right."

Then she smiled kindly at him.

"My dear boy, I know exactly how you feel. That it's all very well for you and Deborah and the young generally to run risks, but that the mere middle-aged must be shielded. All complete nonsense, because if anyone is going to be liquidated it is much better it should be the middle-aged who have had the best part of their lives. Anyway, stop looking upon me as that sacred object, Deborah's mother, and just tell me what dangerous and unpleasant job there is for me to do."

"You know," said the young man with enthusiasm, "I think you're splendid, simply splendid."

"Cut out the compliments," said Tuppence. "I'm admiring myself a good deal, so there's no need for you to chime in. What exactly *is* the big idea?"

Tony indicated the mass of crumpled material with a gesture.

"That," he said, "is the remains of a parachute."

"Aha," said Tuppence. Her eyes sparkled.

"There was just an isolated parachutist," went on Marsdon "Fortunately the L.D.V.'s around here are quite a bright lot. The descent was spotted, and they got her."

"*Her?*"

"Yes, *her!* Woman dressed as a hospital nurse."

"I'm sorry she wasn't a nun," said Tuppence. "There have been so many good stories going around about nuns paying their fares in buses with hairy muscular arms."

"Well, she wasn't a nun and she wasn't a man in disguise. She was a woman of medium height, middle-aged, with dark hair and of slight build."

"In fact," said Tuppence, "a woman not unlike me?"

"You've hit it exactly," said Tony.

"Well?" said Tuppence.

Marsdon said slowly:

"The next part of it is up to you."

Tuppence smiled. She said:

"I'm *on* all right. Where do I go and what do I do?"

"I say, Mrs. Beresford, you really *are* a sport. Magnificent nerve you've got."

"Where do I go and what do I do?" repeated Tuppence impatiently.

"The instructions are very meagre, unfortunately. In the woman's pocket there was a piece of paper with these words on it in German: 'Walk at Leatherbarrow—due east from the stone cross. 14 St. Asalph's Road. Dr. Binion.' "

Tuppence looked up. On the hill top near by was a stone cross.

"That's it," said Tony. "Signposts have been removed, of course. But Leatherbarrow's a biggish place and walking due east from the cross you're bound to strike it."

"How far?"

"Five miles at least."

Tuppence made a slight grimace.

"Healthy walking exercise before lunch," she commented. "I hope Dr. Binion offers me lunch when I get there."

"Do you know German, Mrs. Beresford?"

"Hotel variety only. I shall have to be firm about speaking English—say my instructions were to do so."

"It's an awful risk," said Marsdon.

"Nonsense. Who's to imagine there's been a substitution? Or does everyone know for miles round that there's been a parachutist brought down?"

"The two L.D.V. men who reported it are being kept by the Chief Constable. Don't want to risk their telling their friends how clever they have been!"

"Somebody else may have seen it—or heard about it?"

Tony smiled.

"My dear Mrs. Beresford, every single day, word goes round that one, two, three, four, up to a hundred parachutists have been seen!"

"That's probably quite true," agreed Tuppence. "Well, lead me to it."

Tony said:

"We've got the kit here—and a policewoman who's an expert in the art of makeup. Come with me."

Just inside the copse there was a tumble-down shed. At the door of it was a competent looking middle-aged woman. She looked at Tuppence and nodded approvingly.

Inside the shed, seated on an upturned packing case, Tuppence submitted herself to expert ministrations. Finally the operator stood back, nodded approvingly and remarked:

"There now, I think we've made a very nice job of it. What do you think, sir?"

"Very good indeed," said Tony.

Tuppence stretched out her hand and took the mirror the other woman held. She surveyed her own face earnestly and could hardly repress a cry of surprise.

The eyebrows had been trimmed to an entirely different shape, altering the whole expression. Small pieces of adhesive plaster hidden by curls pulled forward over the ears had tightened the skin of the face and altered its contours. A small amount of nose putty had altered the shape of the nose, giving Tuppence an unexpectedly beaklike profile. Skilful makeup had added several years to her age, with heavy lines running down each side of the mouth. The whole face had a complacent, rather foolish look.

"It's frightfully clever," said Tuppence admiringly. She touched her nose gingerly.

"You must be careful," the other woman warned her. She produced two slices of thin india-rubber. "Do you think you could bear to wear these in your cheeks?"

"I suppose I shall have to," said Tuppence gloomily.

She slipped them in and worked her jaws carefully.

"It's not really too uncomfortable," she had to admit.

Tony then discreetly left the shed and Tuppence shed her own clothing and got into the nurse's kit. It was not too bad a fit, though inclined to strain a little over the shoulders. The dark blue bonnet put the final touch to her new personality. She rejected, however, the stout square-toed shoes.

"If I've got to walk five miles," she said decidedly, "I'll do it in my own shoes."

They both agreed that this was reasonable—particularly as Tuppence's own shoes were dark blue brogues that went well with the uniform.

She looked with interest into the dark blue handbag—powder—no lipstick—two pounds fourteen and sixpence in English money, a handkerchief and an identity card in the name of Freda Elton, 4 Manchester Road, Sheffield.

Tuppence transferred her own powder and lipstick and stood up, prepared to set out.

Tony Marsdon turned his head away. He said gruffly:

"I feel a swine letting you do this."

"I know just how you feel."

"But, you see, it's absolutely vital—that we should get some idea of just where and how the attack will come."

Tuppence patted him on the arm.

"Don't worry, my child. Believe it or not, I'm enjoying myself."

Tony Marsdon said again:

"I think you're simply wonderful!"

THREE

Somewhat weary, Tuppence stood outside 14 St. Asalph's Road and noted that Dr. Binion was a dental surgeon and not a doctor.

From the corner of her eye she noted Tony Marsdon. He was sitting in a racy looking car outside a house further down the street.

It had been judged necessary for Tuppence to walk to Leatherbarrow exactly as instructed, since if she had been driven there in a car the fact might have been noted.

It was certainly true that two enemy aircraft had passed over the downs, circling low before making off, and they could have noted the nurse's lonely figure walking across country.

Tony, with the expert policewoman, had driven off in the opposite direction and had made a big detour before

approaching Leatherbarrow and taking up his position in
St. Asalph's Road.

Everything was now set.

"The arena doors open," murmured Tuppence. "Enter
one Christian en route for the lions. Oh, well, nobody can
say I'm not seeing life."

She crossed the road and rang the bell, wondering as she
did so, exactly how much Deborah liked that young man.

The door was opened by an elderly woman with a stolid
peasant face—not an English face.

"Dr. Binion?" said Tuppence.

The woman looked her slowly up and down.

"You will be Nurse Elton, I suppose."

"Yes."

"Then you will come up to the doctor's surgery."

She stood back, the door closed behind Tuppence, who
found herself standing in a narrow linoleum lined hall.

The maid preceded her upstairs and opened a door on
the next floor.

"Please to wait. The doctor will come to you."

She went out, shutting the door behind her.

A very ordinary dentist's surgery—the appointments
somewhat old and shabby.

Tuppence looked at the dentist's chair and smiled to think
that for once it held none of the usual terrors. She had the
"dentist feeling" all right—but from quite different causes.

Presently the door would open and "Dr. Binion" would
come in. Who would Dr. Binion be? A stranger? Or someone she had seen before? If it was the person she was half
expecting to see—

The door opened.

The man who entered was not at all the person Tuppence
had half fancied she might see! It was someone she had
never considered as a likely starter.

It was Commander Haydock.

14

A flood of wild surmises as to the part Commander Haydock had played in Tommy's disappearance surged through Tuppence's brain, but she thrust them resolutely aside. This was a moment for keeping all her wits about her.

Would or would not the Commander recognize her? It was an interesting question.

She had so steeled herself beforehand to display no recognition or surprise herself, no matter whom she might see, that she felt reasonably sure that she herself had displayed no signs untoward to the situation.

She rose now to her feet and stood there, standing in a respectful attitude, as befitted a mere German woman in the presence of a Lord of creation.

"So you have arrived," said the Commander.

He spoke in English and his manner was precisely the same as usual.

"Yes," said Tuppence, and added, as though presenting her credentials: "Nurse Elton."

Haydock smiled as though at a joke.

"Nurse Elton! Excellent."

He looked at her approvingly.

"You look absolutely right," he said kindly.

Tuppence inclined her head, but said nothing. She was leaving the initiative to him.

"You know, I suppose, what you have to do?" went on Haydock. "Sit down, please."

Tuppence sat down obediently. She replied:

"I was to take detailed instructions from you."

"Very proper," said Haydock. There was a faint suggestion of mockery in his voice.

He said:

"You know the day?"

Tuppence made a rapid decision.

"The fourth!"

Haydock looked startled. A heavy frown creased his forehead.

"So you know that, do you?" he muttered.

There was a pause, then Tuppence said:

"You will tell me, please, what I have to do?"

Haydock said:

"All in good time, my dear."

He paused a minute and then asked:

"You have heard, no doubt, of Sans Souci?"

"No," said Tuppence.

"You haven't?"

"No," said Tuppence firmly.

"Let's see how you deal with that one!" she thought.

There was a queer smile on the Commander's face. He said:

"So you haven't heard of Sans Souci? That surprises me very much—since I was under the impression, you know, *that you'd been living there for the last month . . .*"

There was a dead silence. The Commander said:

"What about that, Mrs. Blenkensop?"

"I don't know what you mean, Dr. Binion. I landed by parachute this morning."

Again Haydock smiled—definitely an unpleasant smile. He said:

"A few yards of canvas thrust into a bush create a wonderful illusion. And I am not Dr. Binion, dear lady. Dr. Binion is, officially, my dentist—he is good enough to lend me his surgery now and again."

"Indeed?" said Tuppence.

"Indeed, Mrs. Blenkensop! Or perhaps you would prefer me to address you by your real name of Beresford?"

Again there was a poignant silence. Tuppence drew a deep breath.

Haydock nodded.

"The game's up, you see. *'You've walked into my parlour,' said the spider to the fly.'*"

There was a faint click and a gleam of blue steel showed in his hand. His voice took on a grim note as he said:

"And I shouldn't advise you to make any noise or try to arouse the neighbourhood! You'd be dead before you got so much as a yelp out, and even if you did manage to scream it wouldn't arouse attention. Patients under gas, you know, often cry out."

Tuppence said composedly:

"You seem to have thought of everything. Has it occurred to you that I have friends who know where I am?"

"Ah! Still harping on the blue-eyed boy—actually brown eyed! Young Antony Marsdon. I'm sorry, Mrs. Beresford, but young Antony happens to be one of our most stalwart supporters in this country. As I said just now, a few yards of canvas creates a wonderful effect. You swallowed the parachute idea quite easily."

"I don't see the point of all this rigmarole!"

"Don't you? We don't want your friends to trace you too easily, you see. *If* they pick up your trail it will lead to Yarrow and to a man in a car. The fact that a hospital nurse, of quite different facial appearance, walked into Leatherbarrow between one and two will hardly be connected with your disappearance."

"Very elaborate," said Tuppence.

Haydock said:

"I admire your nerve, you know. I admire it very much. I'm sorry to have to coerce you—but it's vital that we should know just exactly how much you *did* discover at Sans Souci."

Tuppence did not answer.

Haydock said quietly:

"I'd advise you, you know, to come clean. There are certain—possibilities—in a dentist's chair and instruments."

Tuppence merely threw him a scornful look.

Haydock leaned back in his chair. He said slowly:

"Yes—I daresay you've got a lot of fortitude—your type often has. But what about the other half of the picture?"

"What do you mean?"

"I'm talking about Thomas Beresford, your husband, who has lately been living at Sans Souci under the name of Mr. Meadowes, and who is now very conveniently trussed up in the cellar of my house."

Tuppence said sharply:

"I don't believe it."

"Because of the Penny Playne letter? Don't you realize that that was just a smart bit of work on the part of young Antony. You played into his hands nicely when you gave him the code."

Tuppence's voice trembled.

"Then Tommy—then Tommy—"

"Tommy," said Commander Haydock, "is where he has been all along—completely in my power! It's up to you now. If you answer my questions satisfactorily, there's a chance for him. If you don't—well, the original plan holds. He'll be knocked on the head, taken out to sea and put overboard."

Tuppence was silent for a minute or two—then she said:

"What do you want to know?"

"I want to know who employed you, what your means of communication with that person or persons are, what you have reported so far, and exactly what you know."

Tuppence shrugged her shoulders.

"I could tell you what lies I chose," she pointed out.

"No, because I shall proceed to test what you say." He drew his chair a little nearer. His manner was now definitely appealing—"My dear woman—I know just what you feel about it all, but do believe me when I say I really do admire both you and your husband immensely. You've got grit and pluck. It's people like you who will be needed in the new State—the State that will arise in this country when your present imbecile Government is vanquished. We want to turn some of our enemies into friends—those that are worth while. If I have to give the order that ends your husband's life, I shall do it—it's my duty—but I shall feel really badly about having to do it! He's a fine fellow—quiet, unassuming and clever. Let me impress upon you what so few people in this country seem to understand. Our Leader does not intend to conquer this country in the sense that you all think. He aims at creating a new Britain—a Britain strong in its own power—ruled over, *not* by Germans, but by *Englishmen*. And the best *type* of Englishmen—Englishmen with brains and breeding and courage. *A brave new world*, as Shakespeare puts it."

He leaned forward.

"We want to do away with muddle and inefficiency. With bribery and corruption. With self-seeking and money-grubbing—*and in this new state we want people like you and your husband*—brave and resourceful—enemies that that have been, friends to be. You would be surprised if you knew how many there are in this country, as in others, who have sympathy with and belief in our aims. Among us all we will create a new Europe—a Europe of peace and progress. Try and see it that way—because, I assure you— it *is* that way . . ."

His voice was compelling, magnetic. Leaning forward, he looked the embodiment of a straightforward British sailor.

Tuppence looked at him and searched her mind for a telling phrase. She was only able to find one that was both childish and rude.

"*Goosey, goosey gander!*" said Tuppence. . . .

TWO

The effect was so magical that she was quite taken aback.

Haydock jumped to his feet, his face went dark purple with rage, and in a second all likeness to a hearty British sailor had vanished. She saw what Tommy had once seen— an infuriated Prussian.

He swore at her fluently in German. Then, changing to English, he shouted:

"You infernal little fool! Don't you realize you give youself away completely answering like that? You've done for yourself now—you and your precious husband."

Raising his voice he called:

"Anna!"

The woman who had admitted Tuppence came into the room. Haydock thrust the pistol into her hand.

"Watch her. Shoot if necessary."

He stormed out of the room.

Tuppence looked appealingly at Anna, who stood in front of her with an impressive face.

"Would you really shoot me?" said Tuppence.

Anna answered quietly:

"You need not try to get round me. In the last war my son was killed, my Otto. I was thirty-eight, then—I am sixty-two now—but I have not forgotten."

Tuppence looked at the broad, impassive face. It reminded her of the Polish woman, Vanda Polonska. That same frightening ferocity and singleness of purpose. Motherhood—unrelenting! So, no doubt, felt many a quiet Mrs. Jones and Mrs. Smith all over England. There was no arguing with the female of the species—the mother deprived of her young.

Something stirred in the recesses of Tuppence's brain—some nagging recollection—something that she had always known but had never succeeded in getting into the forefront of her mind. Solomon—Solomon came into it somewhere . . .

The door opened. Commander Haydock came back into the room.

He howled out, beside himself with rage:

"Where is it? Where have you hidden it?"

Tuppence stared at him. She was completely taken aback. What he was saying did not make sense to her.

She had taken nothing and hidden nothing.

Haydock said to Anna:

"Get out."

The woman handed the pistol to him and left the room promptly.

Haydock dropped into a chair and seemed to be striving to pull himself together. He said:

"You can't get away with it, you know. I've got you—and I've got ways of making people speak—not pretty ways.

You'll have to tell the truth in the end. Now then, *what have you done with it?*"

Tuppence was quick to see that here, at least, was something that gave her the possibility of bargaining. If only she could find out what it was she was supposed to have in her possession.

She said cautiously:

"How do you know I've got it?"

"From what you said, you damned little fool. You haven't got it on you—that we know, since you changed completely into this kit."

"Suppose I posted it to someone?" said Tuppence.

"Don't be a fool. Everything you posted since yesterday has been examined. You didn't post it. No, there's only one thing you *could* have done. Hidden it in Sans Souci before you left this morning. I give you just three minutes to tell me where that hiding place is."

He put his watch down on the table.

"*Three minutes, Mrs. Thomas Beresford.*"

The clock on the mantelpiece ticked.

Tuppence sat quite still with a blank impassive face.

It revealed nothing of the racing thoughts behind it.

In a flash of bewildering light she saw everything—saw the whole business revealed in terms of blinding clarity and realized at last who was the centre and pivot of the whole organization.

It came quite as a shock to her when Haydock said:

"Ten seconds more . . ."

Like one in a dream she watched him, saw the pistol arm rise, heard him count:

"One, two, three, four, five—"

He had reached *eight* when the shot rang out and he collapsed forward on his chair, an expression of bewilderment on his broad red face. So intent had he been on watching his victim that he had been unaware of the door behind him slowly opening.

In a flash Tuppence was on her feet. She pushed her way past the uniformed men in the doorway, and seized on a tweed clad arm.

"*Mr. Grant.*"

"Yes, yes, my dear, it's all right now—you've been wonderful—"

Tuppence brushed aside these reassurances.

"*Quick!* There's no time to lose. You've got a car here?"

"Yes." He stared.

"A fast one? We must get to Sans Souci *at once*. If only we're in time. Before they telephone here, and get no answer."

Two minutes later they were in the car, and it was threading its way through the streets of Leatherbarrow. Then they were out in the open country and the needle of the speedometer was rising.

Mr. Grant asked no questions. He was content to sit quietly whilst Tuppence watched the speedometer in an agony of apprehension. The chauffeur had been given his orders and he drove with all the speed of which the car was capable.

Tuppence spoke only once.

"Tommy?"

"Quite all right. Released half an hour ago."

She nodded.

Now, at last, they were nearing Leahampton. They darted and twisted through the town, up the hill.

Tuppence jumped out and she and Mr. Grant ran up the drive. The hall door, as usual, was open. There was no one in sight. Tuppence ran lightly up the stairs.

She just glanced inside her own room in passing, and noted the confusion of open drawers and disordered bed. She nodded and passed on, along the corridor and into the room occupied by Mr. and Mrs. Cayley.

The room was empty. It looked peaceful and smelled slightly of medicines.

Tuppence ran across to the bed and pulled at the coverings.

They fell to the ground and Tuppence ran her hand under the mattress. She turned triumphantly to Mr. Grant with a tattered child's picture book in her hand.

"Here you are. It's all in here—"

"What on—"

They turned. Mrs. Sprot was standing in the doorway staring.

"And now," said Tuppence, *"let me introduce you to M! Yes Mrs. Sprot!* I ought to have known it all along."

It was left to Mrs. Cayley, arriving in the doorway a moment later, to introduce the appropriate anticlimax.

"Oh, *dear,"* said Mrs. Cayley, looking with dismay at her spouse's dismantled bed. "Whatever *will* Mr. Cayley say?"

15

"I ought to have known it all along," said Tuppence.

She was reviving her shattered nerves by a generous tot of old brandy, and was beaming alternately at Tommy and at Mr. Grant—and at Albert, who was sitting in front of a pint of beer and grinning from ear to ear.

"Tell us all about it, Tuppence," urged Tommy.

"You first," said Tuppence.

"There's not much for me to tell," said Tommy. "Sheer accident let me into the secret of the wireless transmitter. I thought I'd got away with it, but Haydock was too smart for me."

Tuppence nodded and said:

"He telephoned to Mrs. Sprot at once. And she ran out into the drive and lay in wait for you with the hammer. She was only away from the bridge table for about three minutes. I *did* notice she was a little out of breath—but I never suspected her."

"After that," said Tommy, "the credit belongs entirely to Albert. He came sniffing round like a faithful dog. I did some impassioned Morse snoring and he cottoned on to it. He went off to Mr. Grant with the news and the two of them came back late that night. More snoring! Result was, I agreed to remain put so as to catch the sea forces when they arrived."

Mr. Grant added his quota.

"When Haydock went off this morning, our people took

charge at Smugglers' Rest. We nabbed the boat this evening."

"And now, Tuppence," said Tommy. "Your story."

"Well, to begin with, I've been the most frightful fool all along! I suspected everybody here except Mrs. Sprot! I *did* once have a terrible feeling of menace, as though I was in danger—that was after I overheard that telephone message about the 4th of the month. There were three people there at the time—I put down my feeling of apprehension to either Mrs. Perenna or Mrs. O'Rourke. Quite wrong—it was the colourless Mrs. Sprot who was the really dangerous personality.

"I went muddling on, as Tommy knows, until after he disappeared. Then I was just cooking up a plan with Albert when suddenly, out of the blue, Antony Marsdon turned up. It seemed all right to begin with—the usual sort of young man that Deb often has in tow. But two things made me think a bit. First, I became more and more sure as I talked to him that I *hadn't* seen him before and that he never *had* been to the flat. The second was that, though he seemed to know all about *my* working at Leahampton, he assumed that *Tommy* was in Scotland. Now that seemed all wrong. If he knew about anyone, it would be *Tommy* he knew about, since I was more or less unofficial. That struck me as very odd.

"Mr. Grant had told me that Fifth Columnists were everywhere—in the most unlikely places. So why shouldn't one of them be working in Deborah's show? I wasn't convinced, but I *was* suspicious enough to lay a trap for him. I told him that Tommy and I had fixed up a code for communicating with each other. Our real one, of course, was a Bonzo postcard, but I told Antony a fairy tale about the *Penny Plain, Twopence Coloured* saying.

"As I hoped, he rose to it beautifully! I got a letter this morning which gave him away completely.

"The arrangements had been all worked out beforehand. All I had to do was to ring up a tailor and cancel a fitting. That was an intimation that the fish had risen."

"Coo-er!" said Albert. "It didn't half give me a turn. I drove up with a baker's van and we dumped a pool of stuff just outside the gate. Aniseed, it was—or smelled like it."

"And then"—Tuppence took up the tale—"I came out and walked in it. Of course it was easy for the baker's van to follow me to the station and someone came up behind me and heard me book to Yarrow. It was after that that it might have been difficult."

"The dogs followed the scent well," said Mr. Grant. "They picked it up at Yarrow station and again on the track the tire had made after you rubbed your shoe on it. It led us down to the copse and up again to the stone cross and after you where you had walked over the downs. The enemy had no idea we could follow you easily after they themselves had seen you start and driven off themselves."

"All the same," said Albert, "it gives me a turn. Knowing you were in that house and not knowing what might come to you. Got in a back window, we did, and nabbed the foreign woman as she came down the stairs. Come in just in the nick of time, we did."

"I knew you'd come," said Tuppence. "The thing was for me to spin things out as long as I could. I'd have pretended to tell if I hadn't seen the door opening. What was really exciting was the way I suddenly saw the whole thing and what a fool I'd been."

"How did you see it?" asked Tommy.

"*Goosey, goosey gander,*" said Tuppence promptly. "When I said that to Commander Haydock he went absolutely livid. And not just because it was silly and crude. No, I saw at once that it *meant* something to him. And then there was the expression on that woman's face—Anna—it was like the Polish woman's and then, of course, I thought of Solomon and I saw the whole thing."

Tommy gave a sigh of exasperation.

"Tuppence, if you say that once again, I'll shoot you myself. Saw all *what?* And what on earth has Solomon got to do with it?"

"Do you remember that two women came to Solomon with a baby and both said it was hers, but Solomon said, 'Very well, cut it in two.' And the false mother said, 'All right.' But the real mother said, 'No, let the other woman

have it.' You see, she couldn't face her child being killed.
Well, that night that Mrs. Sprot shot the other woman, you
all said what a miracle it was and how easily she might
have shot the child. Of course, it ought to have been quite
plain then! If it *had* been her child, she *couldn't* have risked
that shot for a minute. It meant that Betty *wasn't* her child.
And that's why she absolutely *had* to shoot the other
woman."

"Why?"

"Because, of course, the other woman was *the child's
real mother.*" Tuppence's voice shook a little.

"Poor thing—poor hunted thing. She came over a
penniless refugee and gratefully agreed to let Mrs. Sprot
adopt her baby."

"Why did Mrs. Sprot want to adopt the child?"

"*Camouflage!* Supreme psychological camouflage. You
just can't conceive of a master spy dragging her kid into the
business. That's the main reason why I never considered
Mrs. Sprot seriously. Simply because of the child. But
Betty's real mother had a terrible hankering for her baby
and she found out Mrs. Sprot's address and came down
here. She hung about waiting for her chance, and at last
she got it and went off with the child.

"Mrs. Sprot, of course, was frantic. At all costs she
didn't want the police. So she wrote that message and pretended she found it in her bedroom, and roped in Commander Haydock to help. Then, when we'd tracked down
the wretched woman, she was taking no chances and shot
her. . . . Far from not knowing anything about firearms,
she was a very fine shot! Yes, she killed that wretched
woman—and because of that I've no pity for her. She was
bad through and through."

Tuppence paused, then she went on:

"Another thing that ought to have given me a hint was
the likeness between Vanda Polonska and Betty. It was
Betty the woman reminded me of all along. And then the
child's absurd play with my shoe-laces. How much more
likely that she's seen her so-called mother do that—not Carl
von Deinim! But as soon as Mrs. Sprot saw what the child

was doing, she planted a lot of evidence in Carl's room for us to find and added the master touch of a shoe-lace dipped in secret ink.

"I'm glad that Carl wasn't in it," said Tommy. "I liked him."

"He's not been shot, has he?" asked Tuppence anxiously, noting the past tense.

Mr. Grant shook his head.

"He's all right," he said. "As a matter of fact I've got a little surprise for you there."

Tuppence's face lit up as she said:

"I'm terribly glad—for Sheila's sake! Of course we were idiots to go on barking up the wrong tree after Mrs. Perenna."

"She was mixed up in some I.R.A. activities, nothing more," said Mr. Grant.

"I suspected Mrs. O'Rourke a little—and sometimes the Cayleys—"

"And I suspected Bletchley," put in Tommy

"And all the time," said Tuppence, "it was that milk and water creature we just thought of as—Betty's mother."

"Hardly milk and water," said Mr. Grant. "A very dangerous woman and a very clever actress. And, I'm sorry to say, English by birth."

Tuppence said:

"Then I've no pity or admiration for her—it wasn't even her country she was working for." She looked with fresh curiosity at Mr. Grant. "You found what you wanted?"

Mr. Grant nodded.

"It was all in that battered set of duplicate children's books."

"The ones that Betty said were *nasty*," Tuppence exclaimed.

"They *were* nasty," said Mr. Grant drily. *"Little Jack Horner* contained very full details of our naval dispositions. *Johnny Head in Air* did the same for the Air Force. Military matters were appropriately embodied in *There Was a Little Man and He Had a Little Gun."*

"And *Goosey, Goosey Gander?"* asked Tuppence.

Mr. Grant said:

"Treated with the appropriate reagent, that book contains, written in invisible ink, a full list of all prominent personages who are pledged to assist an invasion of this country. Amongst them were two Chief Constables, an Air Vice-Marshal, two Generals, the Head of an Armaments Works, a Cabinet Minister, many Police Superintendents, Commanders of Local Volunteer Defense Organizations, and various military and naval lesser fry, as well as members of our own Intelligence Force."

Tommy and Tuppence stared.

"Incredible!" said the former.

Grant shook his head.

"You do not know the force of the German propaganda. It appeals to something in man, some desire or lust for power. These people were ready to betray their country not for money, but in a kind of megalomaniacal pride in what they, *they themselves*, were going to achieve for that country. In every land it has been the same. It is the Cult of Lucifer—Lucifer, Son of the Morning. Pride and a desire for *personal glory!*"

He added:

"You can realize that, with such persons to issue contradictory orders and confuse operations, the threatened invasion would have had every chance to succeed."

"And now?" said Tuppence.

Mr. Grant smiled.

"And now," he said, *"let them come! We'll be ready for them!"*

16

"Darling," said Deborah. "Do you know I almost thought the most terrible things about you?"

"Did you?" said Tuppence. "When?"

Her eyes rested affectionately on her daughter's dark head.

"That time when you sloped off to Scotland to join father and I thought you were with Aunt Gracie. I almost thought you were having an affair with someone."

"Oh, Deb, did you?"

"Not really, of course. Not at your age. And, of course, I know you and Carrot Top are devoted to each other. It was really an idiot called Tony Marsdon who put it into my head. Do you know, mother—I think I might tell you—he was found afterwards to be a Fifth Columnist. He always did talk rather oddly—how things would be just the same, perhaps better, if Hitler did win."

"Did you—er—like him at all?"

"Tony? Oh, no—he was always rather a bore. I must dance this."

She floated away in the arms of a fair-haired young man, smiling up at him sweetly. Tuppence followed their revolutions for a few minutes, then her eyes shifted to where a tall young man in Air Force uniform was dancing with a fair-haired slender girl.

"I do think, Tommy," said Tuppence, "that our children are rather nice."

"Here's Sheila," said Tommy.

He got up as Sheila Perenna came towards their table.

She was dressed in an emerald evening dress which showed up her dark beauty. It was a sullen beauty tonight and she greeted her host and hostess somewhat ungraciously.

"I've come, you see," she said, "as I promised. But I can't think why you wanted to ask me."

"Because we like you," said Tommy, smiling.

"Do you really?" said Sheila. "I can't think why. I've been perfectly foul to you both."

She paused and murmured:

"But I am grateful."

Tuppence said:

"We must find a nice partner to dance with you."

"I don't want to dance. I loathe dancing. I came just to see you two."

"You will like the partner we've asked to meet you," said Tuppence, smiling.

"I—" Sheila began. Then stopped—for Carl von Deinim was walking across the floor.

Sheila looked at him like one dazed. She muttered:

"You—"

"I, myself," said Carl.

There was something a little different about Carl von Deinim this evening. Sheila stared at him, a trifle perplexed. The colour had come up in her cheeks, turning them a deep glowing red.

She said a little breathlessly:

"I knew that you would be all right now—but I thought they would still keep you interned?"

Carl shook his head.

"There is no reason to intern me."

He went on.

"You have got to forgive me, Sheila, for deceiving you. I am not, you see, Carl von Deinim at all. I took his name for reasons of my own."

He looked questioningly at Tuppence, who said:

"Go ahead. Tell her."

"Carl von Deinim was my friend. I knew him in England some years ago. I renewed acquaintanceship with him in Germany just before the war. I was there then on special business for this country."

"You were in the Intelligence?" asked Sheila.

"Yes. When I was there, queer things began to happen. Once or twice I had some very near escapes. My plans were known when they should not have been known. I realized that there was something very wrong and that 'the rot,' to express it in their terms, had penetrated actually into the service in which I was. I had been let down by my own people. Carl and I had a certain superficial likeness (my Grandmother was a German), hence my suitability for work in Germany. Carl was not a Nazi. He was interested solely in his job—a job I myself had also practised—research chemistry. He decided, shortly before war broke out, to escape to England. His brothers had been sent to concentration camps. There would, he thought, be great difficulties in the way of his own escape, but in an almost miraculous fashion all these difficulties smoothed themselves out. The fact, when he mentioned it to me, made me somewhat suspicious. Why were the authorities making it so easy for von Deinim to leave Germany when his brothers and other relations were in concentration camps and he himself was suspected because of his anti-Nazi sympathies? It seemed as though they wanted him in England for some reason. My own position was becoming increasingly precarious. Carl's lodgings were in the same house as mine and one day I found him, to my sorrow, lying dead on his bed. He had succumbed to depression and taken his own life, leaving a letter behind which I read and pocketed.

"I decided then to effect a substitution. I wanted to get out of Germany—and I wanted to know why Carl was being encouraged to do so. I dressed his body in my clothes and laid it on my bed. It was disfigured by the shot he had fired into his head. My landlady, I knew, was semi-blind.

"With Carl von Deinim's papers I travelled to England and went to the address to which he had been recommended to go. That address was Sans Souci.

"Whilst I was there I played the part of Carl von Deinim and never relaxed. I found arrangements had been made for me to work in the chemical factory there. At first I thought that the idea was I should be compelled to do work for the Nazis. I realized later that the part for which my poor friend had been cast was that of scapegoat.

"When I was arrested on faked evidence, I said nothing. I wanted to leave the revelation of my own identity as late as possible. I wanted to see what would happen.

"It was only a few days ago that I was recognized by one of our people and the truth came out."

Sheila said reproachfully:

"You should have told me."

He said gently:

"If you feel like that—I am sorry."

His eyes looked into hers. She looked at him angrily and proudly—then the anger melted. She said:

"I suppose you had to do what you did. . . ."

"Darling—"

He caught himself up.

"Come and dance. . . ."

They moved off together.

Tuppence sighed.

"What's the matter?" said Tommy.

"I do hope Sheila will go on caring for him now that he isn't a German outcast with everyone against him."

"She looks as though she cared all right."

"Yes, but the Irish are terribly perverse. And Sheila is a born rebel."

"Why did he search your room that day? That's what led us up the garden path so terribly."

Tommy gave a laugh.

"I gather he thought Mrs. Blenkensop wasn't a very convincing person. In fact—while we were suspecting him he was suspecting us."

"Hullo, you two," said Derek Beresford as he and his partner danced past his parents' table. "Why don't you come and dance?"

He smiled encouragingly at them.

"They are so kind to us, bless 'em," said Tuppence.

Presently the twins and their partners returned and sat down.

Derek said to his father:

"Glad you got a job all right. Not very interesting I suppose?"

"Mainly routine," said Tommy.

"Never mind, you're doing something. That's the great thing."

"And I'm glad mother was allowed to go and work, too," said Deborah. "She looks ever so much happier. It wasn't too dull, was it mother?"

"I didn't find it at all dull," said Tuppence.

"Good," said Deborah. She added, "When the war's over, I'll be able to tell you something about my job. It's really frightfully interesting, but very confidential."

"How thrilling," said Tuppence.

"Oh, it is! Of course, it's not so thrilling as flying—"

She looked enviously at Derek.

She said, "He's going to be recommended for—"

Derek said quickly:

"Shut up, Deb."

Tommy said:

"Hullo, Derek, what have you been up to?"

"Oh, nothing much—sort of show all of us are doing. Don't know why they pitched on me," murmured the young airman, his face scarlet. He looked as embarrassed as though he had been accussed of the most deadly of sins.

He got up and the fair-haired girl got up, too.

Derek said:

"Mustn't miss any of this—last night of my leave."

"Come on, Charley," said Deborah.

The two of them floated away with their partners.

Tuppence prayed inwardly:

"Oh, let them be safe—don't let anything happen to them. . . ."

She looked up to meet Tommy's eyes. He said, "About that child—shall we?"

"Betty? Oh, Tommy, I'm so glad you've thought of it, too! I thought it was just me being maternal. You really mean it?"

"That we should adopt her? Why not? She's had a raw deal, and it will be fun for us to have something young growing up."

"Oh, Tommy!"

She stretched out her hand and squeezed his. They looked at each other.

"We always do want the same things," said Tuppence happily.

Deborah, passing Derek on the floor, murmured to him:

"Just look at those two—actually holding hands! They're rather sweet, aren't they. We must do all we can to make up to them for having such a dull time in this war. . . ."

Novels of
mystery and suspense
by
AGATHA CHRISTIE

**undisputed First Lady of
Mystery Fiction, with over 200 million
copies of her books sold**

THE BIG FOUR 75c

DOUBLE SIN 60c

THE LABORS OF HERCULES 75c

THE MOUSETRAP 75c

MURDER AFTER HOURS 75c

MURDER AT HAZELMOOR 75c

MURDER IN MESOPOTAMIA 75c

MURDER IN RETROSPECT 60c

THE MYSTERIOUS MR. QUIN 75c

N OR M 75c

POIROT LOSES A CLIENT 75c

THE REGATTA MYSTERY 75c

THERE IS A TIDE 60c

THEY CAME TO BAGHDAD 60c

13 AT DINNER 75c

13 CLUES FOR MISS MARPLE 50c

13 FOR LUCK 75c

THE UNDER DOG AND OTHER STORIES 75c

DELL BOOKS

If you cannot obtain copies of these titles from your local bookseller, just
send the price (plus 15c per copy for handling and postage) to Dell Books,
P.O. Box 1000, Pinebrook, N.J. 07058. No postage or handling charge is
required on any order of five or more books.